Unicorn University
4 Books in 1!

UNICORN
University

4 BOOKS IN 1!

Twilight, Say Cheese!
Sapphire's Special Power
Shamrock's Seaside Sleepover
Comet's Big Win

★ by DAISY SUNSHINE ★
illustrated by MONIQUE DONG

ALADDIN
New York London Toronto Sydney New Delhi

ALADDIN

An imprint of Simon & Schuster Children's Publishing Division
1230 Avenue of the Americas, New York, New York 10020
This Aladdin hardcover edition May 2022
Twilight, Say Cheese! text copyright © 2021 by Simon & Schuster, Inc.
Sapphire's Special Power text copyright © 2021 by Simon & Schuster, Inc.
Shamrock's Seaside Sleepover text copyright © 2021 by Simon & Schuster, Inc.
Comet's Big Win text copyright © 2021 by Simon & Schuster, Inc.
Illustrations copyright © 2021 by Monique Dong
All rights reserved, including the right of reproduction in whole or in part in any form.
ALADDIN and related logo are registered trademarks of Simon & Schuster, Inc.
For information about special discounts for bulk purchases, please contact Simon & Schuster Special Sales
at 1-866-506-1949 or business@simonandschuster.com.
The Simon & Schuster Speakers Bureau can bring authors to your live event. For more information or to
book an event contact the Simon & Schuster Speakers Bureau at 1-866-248-3049 or visit our website
at www.simonspeakers.com.
Series designed by Laura Lyn DiSiena
Cover designed by Alicia Mikles
The illustrations for this book were rendered digitally.
The text of this book was set in Tinos.
Manufactured in the United States of America 0322 FFG
2 4 6 8 10 9 7 5 3 1
Library of Congress Control Number 2021950501
ISBN 9781665921633 (hc)
ISBN 9781534461673 (*Twilight, Say Cheese!* ebook)
ISBN 9781534461703 (*Sapphire's Special Power* ebook)
ISBN 9781534461734 (*Shamrock's Seaside Sleepover* ebook)
ISBN 9781534461765 (*Comet's Big Win* ebook)
These titles were previously published individually.

For lovers of sparkles, rainbows, and magic

CONTENTS

Twilight,
Say Cheese!

1

Ruby-Red Barns

Twilight was having an almost perfect day. The sun was shining, and the yellow buttercups of Sunshine Springs were in full bloom. Her mother had even surprised her with her very favorite breakfast, apple oat muffins with cinnamon sugar. It was a long trip from their farm to Unicorn University, but Twilight's father made it a great adventure and told funny stories and ideas the whole way.

The day was only *almost* perfect because Twilight could not stop thinking about how nervous she was to start school. She worried that she wouldn't know the right things to say or do. Outside her family, she had never spent much time with other unicorns. Her sister Sunset was outgoing, and her sister Dusk was funny. But Twilight had always been shy. How was she going to make friends?

"Look, Twilight! There's Unicorn U!"

Twilight looked up to where her mother's golden horn was pointing. She could see a cluster of big ruby-red barns standing atop the grassy hill in the distance.

Twilight felt her stomach drop. Her nervousness might have just been in the back of her mind on the way there, but now the situation felt very, very real. She felt positively sick.

Twilight thought about telling her parents that she was actually too sick to go to school, but she had decided to make her family proud, swallow her fears, and go. Even if it did make her stomach flip and flop.

"Sugarplum for your thoughts?" Twilight's father asked. He nudged her cheek with his long, gray nose.

"Same old thing, I guess. I'm worried about starting school," Twilight told him.

Twilight's father neighed knowingly. "Of course you are, honey. Everyone is, on their first day, and your sisters were too. But Sunset and Dusk did wonderfully at Unicorn U. You are sure to follow in their hoofprints."

Twilight nodded, though his words didn't actually make her feel any better. When Sunset had been at Unicorn U, she'd been the star of the school hoofball team. Her magical ability let her fly with just a run and a jump, and now she worked with dragons in Cloud Kingdom. Dusk had had the best grades in school and could make flowers grow just by breathing on them. Since graduating, she'd been developing a brand-new apple tree that could grow in any of the five kingdoms.

It was a lot to live up to.

Unlike her sisters, Twilight didn't like to stand out from the crowd. She preferred quiet activities, like reading and painting. Painting was the perfect way to record all her wild daydreams, and books had all the company she could need.

When Twilight had been little, she'd loved reading about magical creatures, especially lions and mice. Lions reminded her of her sisters—always stomping in after practice or conducting experiments. Mice reminded her of herself—quiet and observant. Twilight never minded being the quiet one. She liked watching the goings-on of her house from her favorite spot by the window. It just felt like her role in the family.

That was, until her magical ability had appeared.

She'd discovered it when Dusk had come home one afternoon and jumped from behind a haystack while Twilight had been out in the field, painting and lost in thought. Twilight didn't even realize she had become invisible until Dusk started panicking and yelling for her. Twilight quickly appeared again, just in time to comfort her sister.

Ever since that day, Twilight's invisibility had come and gone unexpectedly. She usually became invisible when she was embarrassed or nervous, but she would always reappear again once her family noticed that she had disappeared, which usually meant she had to whinny or stomp to get their attention. Her parents called her invisibility a magical gift, but Twilight thought of it as a curse. Having to make a spectacle to get a unicorn's attention? That was decidedly too lionlike.

What if I fade out in front of everyone at school? Twilight worried, shuddering at the thought. The last thing she wanted was to be forced to make a scene in front of her classmates.

Twilight's mother trotted over, her well-worn leather satchel swinging gently from her neck. She carried a large pink tulip in her mouth. Carefully she tucked the flower behind Twilight's ear. "You just be yourself, honey," she said.

Twilight let out a soft thank-you neigh, and this time she did feel a little better. She looked down at the ground, and smiled at how her bright purple hooves stood out against her jet-black coat. Dusk had given her a hooficure the night before, to celebrate her first day of school. At first Twilight had worried that it was too flashy, but Dusk convinced her that everyone would have hooficures and that this would help her fit in.

Twilight looked back up at her mom and dad, whose loving smiles gave her a small boost of confidence. Twilight didn't know if she was ready for Unicorn University, but she wanted to try. She stood up straight and smiled back at them.

"Look out, world!" her father neighed merrily. "Twilight is going to school!"

2

Disappearing Act

"I am not going to school," Twilight told her parents. But they were too distracted by the school's impressive grounds to notice.

The three of them had just arrived at the Unicorn University Welcome Picnic on the school's main lawn. This was called the Looping Lawn. It was a large grass-covered hill that connected the Silver Lining Stables, the Crystal Library, and the Wondering Woods.

The Silver Lining Stables, which weren't actually silver but were more like big red barns, were where students would live during the year. Large sliding doors with bright white borders stood open, as if welcoming students inside.

Flower boxes bursting with plants of every color decorated the windows. And a weather vane perched on top of each building. The large metal structures all spun slowly with the wind's changing directions.

"Your stable has the sailboat weather vane on top," Twilight's mother said.

"Same one as Dusk," her fathered remembered. "Sunset was in the stable with the cloud weather vane, which was rather fitting."

Twilight smiled. It was comforting to think of her sisters in this strange new place.

"And that's the library!" her father cheered, motioning toward the building on the other side of the lawn. The castle-like structure sparkled in the distance.

The school was so big and important-looking. It made Twilight feel as if pixies were dancing jigs her in stomach. But her parents were so proud of her, and she didn't want to ruin it by telling them how worried she was. She tried to put on a happy face.

"It looks as if it's really made of crystal," Twilight said.

Her mother laughed softly. "That's because it is!"

Twilight could only stare in wonder. Her sisters had told her about the library, but they tended to exaggerate. Neither of them could resist a good story, and Twilight had learned to take most things they said with a dash of salt. This time it seemed that they hadn't explained enough.

"Come on, you two! There's a party happening!" Twilight's father called over his shoulder as he trotted toward the welcome picnic.

"He's right! Let's go join the fun," Twilight's mother said. She galloped after Twilight's father.

Twilight shook her head. Her parents were outgoing and carefree, and very different from Twilight. At home that felt right. Twilight took care of the little things, and she felt like she was an important part of the family. But here at Unicorn University, with its bright colors and large buildings? It seemed as if she needed a much bigger personality in order to belong. Reluctant and timid, Twilight slowly followed her partying parents.

The center of the Looping Lawn was filled with unicorn

fillies and colts laughing, prancing, and calling out to each other. Sugarplums and candied apples were piled high on a snack table, and a rainbow spelled WELCOME TO UNICORN UNIVERSITY! in big cursive letters over the party. There was a garden-gnome band playing joyful tunes on the stage, their large red pointed hats bouncing in time. Some of the unicorns were dancing to the music, while others were showing off their magical abilities—Twilight even saw one unicorn change her mane from purple to pink to teal. Clearly the other students had no trouble controlling their abilities!

Twilight did not feel as happy as the other unicorns looked. She wasn't sure where to stand or what to do. She shifted from one hoof to the other, wondering how all the other fillies and colts seemed to fit right in.

Maybe the university had made a mistake in accepting her, Twilight worried. There were schools all over Sunshine Springs, but her family always said that Unicorn University was the very best, and it was where everyone in her family had gone. But what if Twilight wasn't the best? What if she didn't belong here? She didn't have any control over her

ability, not like the filly who could easily change the color of her mane. Twilight didn't know the moves to the dances the students were doing, and she had no idea how they could get a rainbow to spell out words. But the very worst part was that everyone was already talking and playing. It seemed like they already knew what to do.

Twilight felt a tingle begin to creep up from her hooves, as if she had stepped into a cool stream on a warm summer's day. She looked down and saw that there was only grass where her hooves should have been. It looked as if she were floating in midair.

Twilight hoped that no one noticed. She didn't want the other unicorns to think she was trying to show off her ability too! She didn't want them to think she was trying to brag, especially when she had no idea how to control her invisibility.

Twilight searched for her parents, but they were across the field, by the baskets of sugarplums, where her dad was in the middle of telling a story and making a group of unicorns laugh. Twilight wanted to run over to them to get their attention or, better yet, run home to the family farm, but her legs were frozen in place. Hot tears of frustration welled up as she felt herself plunge into full invisibility.

Twilight had just started worrying about how long she would have to be an invisible filly-shaped rock when— oof!—an adult unicorn with a multicolored mane ran right into her.

The unicorn chuckled. "Now, I know I bumped into something! But what could it be?" she asked.

Not wanting to be impolite, Twilight squeaked an embarrassed "Hello." She wished and wished she could run all the way home.

The unicorn just smiled and said, "Hello to you too!" She wore a large garland of yellow buttercups and orange poppies around her neck. Her voice was kind and her eyes were warm, and Twilight instantly felt herself relax.

Twilight could feel the tingly invisibility start to fade, replaced by the warm, welcome sunshine feeling of turning visible again. She looked down with cheer to see her purple-painted hooves appear. But she froze again when she saw that the other unicorn was looking at her quizzically.

"Welcome back!" the unicorn said. "What happened just now?" She seemed positive and kind, and it wasn't too long before Twilight found her voice again.

"I've only just discovered my magical ability," Twilight whispered. "I turn invisible when I get nervous."

The unicorn nodded. "It's hard getting used to your new power. I remember those days well. But that's part of the reason why you're here! To learn more about it and to learn to control it."

Twilight was smiling when she looked up to see her mother and father galloping over to them. She could see the concern on their faces as they got closer.

"It's not easy to find your invisible daughter," Twilight's father said, slightly out of breath.

"Professor Sherbet!" Twilight's mother said. "Thank goodness you found Twilight. How wonderful to see you again."

Twilight's large gray eyes went wide in surprise. "Professor Sherbet?" she asked softly. "You wrote my letter of acceptance. You're supposed to be my teacher!" This was not at all the stuffy, scary professor she had imagined.

Professor Sherbet nodded, her wreath of flowers shaking gently. "That's right, Twilight! I'm excited to finally meet you. Welcome to Unicorn University."

"Thank you, Professor," Twilight said quietly.

"I'm very excited to learn about your new ability," Ms. Sherbet said. "What a wonderful thing you can do!"

Twilight felt herself blush. She didn't know what to say.

"I always find the first day and last day to be the hardest," Professor Sherbet told her. "The first because everyone is nervous about making a good impression. And the last because no one wants to say good-bye."

Twilight looked up at the smiling teacher. "You really think everyone is nervous?" she asked.

"I do. Even now, after many years of school and many years of teaching, I'm nervous about meeting a new class. It's always hard to start new things."

That made Twilight feel much more comfortable. Finally it seemed as if someone understood. "I have been pretty nervous about today," she said.

Ms. Sherbet smiled. "I'm sure most of the fillies and colts feel just like you do. Why don't you and your parents go check out the stables? It might make the university feel more like home. You can meet us in the Friendly Fields for our first class afterward. Once we're all gathered, I'll lead you on a tour of the school. Then I'll leave your class for the afternoon so you can create the class picture scene. I have a feeling this will be the best year yet!"

Professor Sherbet trotted off in the direction of the party as Twilight looked up at her parents. "Do you know what picture she was talking about?" she asked them.

Both parents stared back at her with their faces scrunched up. Twilight couldn't tell if they were feeling guilty or concerned. Which made her stomach drop all the way to her hooves. *What else haven't they told me about?*

"Remember, honey?" her mother said gently. "The picture that each of your sisters took on her first day of school?"

Twilight did remember. In their bedroom they each had a framed picture of their class in silly poses. Twilight had just assumed her class would do that later in the year, once they'd all gotten to know each other.

"You see," her father said, "every year the new class takes a group photo that they have to design and stage. It's a way to get to know each other. Everyone shares their ideas, and you all work together. The school always says that each unicorn is supposed to 'let their personality shine through.'"

"Each class approaches it differently," Twilight's mother explained. "My class staged it like a play where we were all acting in a big scene. It was really fun!"

"But on the first day?" Twilight squeaked, her voice much higher pitched than usual. She hadn't been planning on talking at all for at least the first week. She'd been hoping to observe and make a plan. Now she would have to let her personality shine, whatever that meant. A wave of nerves rolled over her. She wished her parents had prepared her for this.

"Don't worry, honey! You'll have fun, I promise," her mother told her.

Twilight looked up at her smiling parents. Once again she could see how excited they were for her to start school. They thought of it as an exciting new experience. How could she explain to them that it only felt like a nightmare?

"Come on," her father said. "Let's go check out the stables like Professor Sherbet suggested."

Twilight tried again to put on her bravest face. She noticed the lawn was sprinkled with little daisies, just like her lawn was back home. The familiar sight made her feel a bit better as they walked over. Soon Twilight and her parents arrived at the entrance of the stable with the sailboat twirling lazily on top.

Twilight entered her new stable with her mom and dad. It was large enough to hold forty stalls, but there was lots of light from the big windows, and the wooden floors were made of mismatched, crooked planks. It was perfectly cozy and inviting. Twilight relaxed when she found that no one else was inside. Looking around, she saw that some students had decorated their stalls with flowers, sparkling rocks, or colorful blankets. One filly had hung up a crystal that cast little rainbows everywhere.

In the acceptance letter, Professor Sherbet had included all the information Twilight would need for school. She would be staying in stall number twelve and would need to bring science goggles, a horn protector, a small cauldron, and a can of hoof ink, as well as a whole bunch of books, such as *The Beginner's Guide to Planting & Potions* and *The History of the Five Kingdoms*.

Now Twilight found the stall with a shiny golden number twelve nailed to the swinging red door. Inside were all the books and materials that her parents had sent ahead, and she saw that everything had already been carefully put away. Twilight wondered who had arranged everything so nicely. It made the stall feel a little more like her own.

Twilight's mother joined her in the stall and bobbed her head to hang her satchel on one of the stall's hooks. Using her glittering horn, she pulled a book out by its shiny brass book ring. Twilight read the title, *Little Unicorns*.

"This was my favorite book when I was your age," Twilight's mother told her, slipping the book onto the stall's book hook. "It's about three sisters, in case you ever get homesick."

Twilight felt a tear fall down her cheek. She was going to miss her parents so much.

Twilight nuzzled her mother's cheek. "Thank you," she said.

"We are very excited for you," her father said.

"And very proud," her mother added.

Twilight felt a familiar pang of worry. She didn't want to disappoint her parents. She wanted to keep making them proud.

The three unicorns huddled together in a Twilight sandwich. No one was ready, but it was time to say good-bye.

3

The Friendly Fields

Twilight left the stables before her parents. She was sure she would start to cry if she watched them walk away, and thought it was best to head straight for class after they said their good-byes.

She turned once more to wave to her parents on the way out. Their smiles and waving golden horns gave her a little confidence as she headed over to class. She tried to ignore the dancing pixies in her stomach as she walked back across the daisy-dotted knolls toward the sign for the Friendly Fields.

"Hey! Wait up!" a voice called from behind her. Twilight stopped and turned to see a mint-green colt trotting up to her. Large glasses were balanced on his nose, and his silver mane flew wildly behind him.

Twilight's chest started pounding. Had she done something wrong already?

"Hi! Are you a first year too? Are you in Ms. Sherbet's class? What's your name? My name is Shamrock!" All the words came tumbling out of his mouth as he bounced up next to her. In his excitement his glasses had gone askew, and his mane lay wildly around his shoulders.

Twilight smiled. There was something about his goofiness and excitement that reminded her of her parents' enthusiasm.

"I'm Twilight," she said. "I'm in Ms. Sherbet's class, and I'm on my way there now." The words rushed out of her so quickly that she surprised herself a little.

"Great! I can't wait for classes to start," he said. "I've been studying all summer!" He started bouncing again. "All the usual subjects of course: math, science, the history of the five kingdoms. I've been trying to learn Gnomish, but I'm afraid I said the wrong thing to the guitar player at the party. I thought I was just saying 'good job,' but I don't think I did it right. . . ."

Twilight didn't know what to say. She hadn't studied at all!

"Glimmer-foot!" Shamrock grumbled, and shook his head. "I've done it again. My dads are always telling me I have to take a breath and remember to ask other unicorns questions, not just blurt out everything I'm thinking. I'm sorry." He paused and did indeed take one deep breath, and let it out slowly. "What did you do this summer?" he asked a little more calmly.

Twilight was at a loss for words. How could she tell him that her stack of schoolbooks would make her nervous every time she looked at them, and she'd ended up covering them with a blanket? All she managed was a shrug and a frown in response.

"You know, most unicorns don't study over the summer," Shamrock went on. "They actually say in the handbook that the summer is a time for regrouping and doing what you love. I just love studying! Did you do what you love?"

Twilight smiled. She had definitely done what she loved over the summer. "I like to read and paint. And I did lots of that."

"You know how to paint?!" Shamrock exclaimed. "Could you teach me?"

Twilight thought about it. "I've never taught anyone before. But I could try."

Shamrock and Twilight followed a winding dirt path through the Wondering Woods. They could see small animals darting through the brush, and could see the bright blue sky through the trees. When they looked back, they spotted the cluster of weather vanes and the top of the Crystal Library peeking over the forest. Shamrock kept the conversation going the whole way, commenting on the school grounds and all that he'd learned about it over the summer. He didn't ask many questions, which was fine by Twilight. She was still so nervous that it felt like her tongue was a Popsicle—completely frozen.

It wasn't long before they were passing through the large wooden gates of the Friendly Fields. And it was easy to find Professor Sherbet and her flower wreath.

Twilight's stomach dropped when she noticed all the students gathered around the professor. They were too many of them!

It seemed like Shamrock was nervous too. He stopped short and looked as if he'd been scared by a ghost.

"Oh *no*! We're late!" he squeaked. "The professor is already speaking! Rule number five in the Unicorn University Handbook clearly says that students must always be on time for class. You have until the third bell rings. But I didn't hear any bell. Did you? Oh no! Do you think we're going to get expelled?"

Twilight's eyes widened, and she gulped. Expelled?

4

The Name Game

"Come! Come! You're just in time!" Professor Sherbet called from the group of unicorns.

Twilight breathed a sigh of relief and looked over to Shamrock. "Guess we're not going to be expelled just yet," she said as they walked over.

Shamrock nodded seriously. "I'm excited to be here, but I'm afraid that I'm going to do something wrong. It's all I've ever wanted, to come here and learn."

Twilight didn't know what to say. She would have liked to stay home forever.

"Welcome, Shamrock and Twilight!" Ms. Sherbet cheered as they reached the group, and everyone turned to look at them. Twilight felt her stomach pixies start dancing again. She *did not* like having all those eyes on her. "Okay. Everyone gather together," Ms. Sherbet continued. "We're going to play a little game to get to know each other."

The class backed up to form a large circle, everyone's horns pointing in. Twilight found a place between Shamrock and a sky-blue unicorn, who was talking with a rose-colored student next to her. Everyone was chatting excitedly with their neighbors.

But Twilight was not excited. She didn't mind playing games at home. In fact, she was the undefeated champion of Pictionary in her house. But today she would have much preferred to stay quiet and listen to everyone else talk.

"This is the way it works," Professor Sherbet went on. "Everyone introduce yourself and tell us something you love that starts with the first letter of your name. For example, my name is Professor *Sherbet*, and I love the *seashells* I find down on the *shore*."

The rose-colored filly raised her sparkling horn and jumped a little. "Oh, Professor! How are we supposed

to choose just one? Do you think I could choose maybe three . . . or four?"

Professor Sherbet neighed merrily. "The point of the game is to help you learn each other's names. I think adding too many facts would confuse things. But I like your enthusiasm, Comet!"

Twilight was impressed. *Comet must have an amazing imagination!* Twilight wondered if Comet was an artist.

But Twilight was happy that the professor had stuck to the original plan. She was having enough trouble deciding on one thing she wanted to share, not to mention three or four! Twilight liked a lot of stuff that began with *T*, but what did she truly *love*? What thing would best describe her to her classmates?

Twilight liked the way *trees* swayed together on a windy day.

She liked when her mom would bring her a bowl of rose *tea* before bed.

She liked the *taste* of rain on hot summer days.

But which of these was the right thing to say?

Twilight was so lost in thought that she didn't realize it was her turn to speak. Shamrock gave her a little nudge.

"Oh, um—hi!" she squeaked. "My name is Twilight, and I love how ocean waves turn a special shade of *teal* when they hit the sand. The color looks just like the glass bottles that line the big window in my kitchen. I like the way colors can do that. Even when you're far away, you can still find the colors of home."

Professor Sherbet smiled at her.

The filly with a sky-blue coat and a braided royal-blue mane spoke up next. "My name is Sapphire, and I love salty seaweed!" she called out.

"My name is Comet, and I love candy!" the rose-colored unicorn said next.

As they went around the circle, Twilight felt herself shrink back. *Everyone else is choosing something simple, and I went on about teal waves,* she worried. She imagined a giant sign that said ODDBALL hanging over her head.

"Wonderful job, everyone!" Professor Sherbet told them after the last student had gone.

"It was lovely getting to know you all a little better. Perhaps it can serve as some inspiration for your class photo!"

The class started talking loudly about the class picture. It seemed like everyone but Twilight was looking forward to it.

Twilight felt as if a cloud were passing over, blocking out the sunshine. Her hooves shimmered out of sight. *Oh no! No, not now*, she thought. She squinted and tried to will the invisibility away.

"Okay. Time for the campus tour. Everyone, follow me!" The professor started galloping away, and the class quickly followed.

Twilight felt the chilly invisibility washing over her. She had totally disappeared!

"But wait!" Shamrock stopped and stretched his neck this way and that. "Where has Twilight gone?" He walked away a little to look into the woods behind him. "Twilight!" he called.

"Shamrock, shhh," Twilight whispered, trying to get him to quiet down. She did not want the rest of the group to come back and not see her like this.

Luckily, it wasn't long at all before the sunshine feeling rushed over her and she fully appeared again.

Twilight blushed. "I'm, um, right here," she told Shamrock.

He quickly turned to see her, tilting his head in surprise. "What happened?"

Twilight's shoulders slumped. "I fade out sometimes. I'm trying to get it under control."

"I don't have a magical ability yet. I wish I had one," Shamrock admitted, scuffing his front hoof on the ground.

Twilight searched for the right words but couldn't think of what to say. Not all unicorns had special abilities. Her mom didn't have one, but her dad had a special way with plants. He just knew what they needed. He always said that he could speak their language. But her mom was amazing with plants too, just in a different way. Usually unicorn

abilities appeared before your first year of school, but sometimes they developed later. Twilight could see that Shamrock
felt left out, but her ability caused her nothing but trouble.
She would rather not have one at all.

After an awkward moment Shamrock tossed his head
toward the rest of their class. "Hey, we'd better catch up
with the group or we really will get expelled!"

Twilight looked after him as he trotted away. It was
the first time another student had seen her ability, and she
wished it had gone better. She wished she knew what she
was supposed to say and do. Staying quiet was definitely not
working here.

Twilight wanted to turn in the other direction and head
back home, but then she thought about her parents and
how excited they were for her to start school. She took a
deep breath and stood a little taller, before galloping after
Shamrock to join the rest of the group.

5

The Crystal Library

Twilight and Shamrock caught up with the group at the Science Stables.

"This is where we'll use our bubbling cauldrons to make healing tonics and potions," Ms. Sherbet was saying. "And in the garden behind this stable, we'll learn all about the plants of Sunshine Springs. But we have much to do today, so we'd better get going!"

Professor Sherbet dashed off again, her class trotting behind her. Twilight thought they looked like a rainbow, the herd of different-colored coats moving together.

They passed by the Gemstone Caves and the Sparkling Quarry, where the older students would have classes.

Twilight's eyes went wide when they made it to the Avocado Arena, a large flat field filled with unicorn students tossing balls and disks of different shapes and sizes between them. To her left was a big sparkling pond where unicorns splashed around. Shouts and laughter carried across the field. Twilight was amazed as she looked around. She had never been much of an athlete and knew only one or two of the games. *Does the rest of the class know how to play all these sports?* she worried.

"We call it the Avocado Arena because of the color of the grass," Professor Sherbet explained. "As you can see, it's the color of an avocado! The grass that our groundskeeper, Mr. Sorrel, uses is extra bouncy, for all the activities we'll do here. You'll all play hoofball, of course, but there are a ton of other games we'll play here as well."

Some of the class whooped in response. Twilight did not feel excited about the idea of hoofball, but she decided to worry about that another day.

"And now for our last stop on the tour. The library!" Ms. Sherbet announced. The class followed her back through the Friendly Fields, through the Wondering Woods, and across the Looping Lawn. They were out of breath when they finally arrived in front of the glimmering rainbow staircase of the Crystal Library.

It was wonderful to see the library up close. Twilight had never seen anything so large and magical. The class came to a stop before a giant, winding staircase that led up to the castle-like building. When she looked up, Twilight could spot four glittering towers on each corner. Windows of every shape were cut into the sides, and a large garden grew all around the walls. Unlike the other buildings on campus, the library wasn't made of wood. Instead it was made up of what looked like large rainbow blocks.

"I heard that this is the biggest library in the whole world!" one filly said.

"Well, that's not true. Everyone knows that the biggest library is in Soaring Spires," Sapphire told them. "This might be the biggest library in Sunshine Springs, though."

The other filly just shrugged.

Twilight was extra timid around Sapphire. Like

Shamrock, Sapphire seemed to know a ton about the school already. Way more than the rest of the class. On top of that, Sapphire didn't seem like she was afraid of anything. Twilight felt like her total opposite.

A hush came over the class as they walked up to the library. Even though they stepped carefully, you could still hear their steps clatter on the rainbow-colored stairs.

"I read in the handbook that artisans from all over the world chiseled thousands of crystals into stackable bricks to create the whole building. It's the hardest substance known to any creature, and it should stand for hundreds of thousands of years," Shamrock whispered to the group.

Twilight gasped at the spectacular doors. Each crystal reflected the light into tiny rainbows. Despite the students' muddy hooves, the stairs remained perfectly clean as the class made their way up to the intricately carved doors.

"The bricks have been enchanted to repel dirt," Shamrock said quietly. "It's another way to ensure that the building—and the books inside it—stays safe."

The sight when they walked through the large, dazzling

doors took Twilight's breath away. She could hear the other students gasp around her. Rows and rows of books circled around the building, all of them hanging by gleaming brass, golden, and silver circles. Balconies full of even more books lined the walls above their heads. Twilight could see that some unicorns were peering down from above to the floors below. The middle of the large first-floor room was filled with long rows of tables. Each table was made of shining brass and dark-colored wood. Already there were large stacks of books laid out in front of students.

For the first time that day, Twilight could picture what her life would be like here at school. She imagined coming here on a quiet afternoon and browsing through all these books. Maybe she could find a cozy corner by a window. She felt light, like she was finally at home.

The class gathered around Professor Sherbet. She had led them to the very middle of the room, where they could see everything. They all stayed perfectly quiet, even though no one had asked them to.

But the silence was soon disrupted by the clatter of

hooves on crystal. Twilight looked up to see a huge, shaggy teal unicorn with a thick raincloud-gray mane trotting toward them.

"Welcome to the library, new students!" the unicorn boomed. He grinned widely as his greeting echoed across the room. It made the whole class smile. Twilight was instantly comfortable around him, somehow. He made the place feel even more welcoming.

"Hello, Professor Jazz!" Professor Sherbet said. "Meet our newest class. Class, this is the librarian, Professor Jazz!"

"Hello, Professor Jazz!" the class said in unison.

"Hello! Hello! And welcome to my library," he boomed again.

Twilight could tell how excited he was to meet them. He bounced a little on his hooves and beamed at each student. His enthusiasm was contagious. Soon everyone was giggling and wiggling as they looked around the room.

"We have every book you could want, and if we don't, just tell me and I'll get it for you. It's my goal to be the largest library in the world!" he said.

"*Told ya,*" Sapphire whispered.

"But first let's do a little introduction." Professor Jazz swung his humongous head and gestured with his horn around the room. "All our books are arranged alphabetically by author and separated by subject. When you take out a book, be sure to tell me, and I can write it down. We like to keep track of our books here at Unicorn U."

Twilight nodded seriously. She felt so very lucky to be in this space, among all these stories. She would always treat the library with respect.

"Now, who has a book they would like to read?" Professor Jazz asked.

Sapphire's horn went right into the air. "I would like to learn how to weave the strongest nets," she said when he called on her. "My family lives by the ocean, and we like to harvest seaweed, of course. I love seaweed, but I hate fixing the ropes. Is there a book about unbreakable nets?"

"Wonderful! Wonderful!" Professor Jazz neighed happily. "This is just what the library is for. Well done, Sapphire!"

Professor Jazz's reaction made everyone start wiggling

again. Horns shot up into the air. All the students were eager to offer their questions too. Twilight even found herself wanting to ask him something. *Maybe there's a book about escaping the class picture*, she thought.

Professor Sherbet neighed in her merry way. "Let's start with this question. You'll have plenty of time to come back," she told them.

"Now, let me think." Professor Jazz tapped his left hoof a few times on the sparkling floor. "First we'll have to find you the strongest rope, which I believe is the Spider Fairy's thread. Though, we will have to confirm. . . . Hmm. Let's get the complete guide to fairy thread to be sure. Then we'll need a weaving book as well. Follow me! Follow me!"

The class followed behind Professor Jazz as he led them to a corner of the library. Twilight hung toward the back of the group, wanting to linger and look closely at every-thing. She peered down the aisles of books and listened to the muffled chatter of students all around her. *How magical*, she thought.

She caught up with the class in time to see Professor Jazz

using his horn to get a large purple book with painted fairy wings on the spine. Then he led the group down another aisle to get a faded blue book with the word "weaving" printed in

big block letters on the cover. Both books hung from gleaming silver rings that now circled his horn.

"I think this will be a good place to start!" He trotted toward the large desk at the back of the library, with the class following quickly behind.

Professor Jazz went behind the desk to a shining silver hook. A little plaque above it said SAPPHIRE. He dipped his horn to slide the books onto the hook. Then he turned back toward the group.

"You all have a hook back here, and if you ever need to put a book on hold, just ask me and it will be waiting for you. After the tour, Sapphire, you can come back and check these out for your project. I'll search for other books in the meantime."

Twilight looked at the wall and spotted her own name above a silver hook. It was like all the other plaques, just a simple silver rectangle. But it gave her a thrill to see her name up there. It made her feel like she might belong here after all.

"Thank you, Mr. Jazz!" Professor Sherbet said. "Now, class, follow me outside—it's time for lunch!"

6

Class Picnic

The Peony Pasture was a large orchard covered with apple trees and, of course, peonies. The older unicorns were gathered in groups around the field, grazing on grass and munching apples. The whole pasture was abuzz with the sounds of neighing, laughter, and excited chatter. Shamrock was talking with Comet and Sapphire as they followed Ms. Sherbet through the trees, and all their other classmates were giggling and discussing the day with each other.

Twilight suddenly felt very small. She was the only one not excited and chatting away. Twilight just felt panicked and sweaty.

Professor Sherbet ushered them over to an open spot under

an old apple tree. She reached up
and used her horn to shake a
bunch of apples loose. "Eat
up, fillies and colts! We have
a big afternoon ahead of us,
and I want you all to have a
good lunch."

"Because of the school
pictures?" Shamrock asked.
He already had a big bite of grass,
and some of the strands were hanging out of his mouth as
he talked. "I know all about them from the handbook," he
added.

"That's right, Shamrock!" Professor Sherbet told him.
"It's a tradition here at Unicorn U to create a unique and
memorable picture. You should all get to know each other
and work together to create something really special. Every
year we give our students one direction: let each student's
personality shine through. This exercise is a great way to get
to know one another."

Twilight felt the stomach pixies, and they were tap-dancing this time. She had hoped Ms. Sherbet would forget about the class picture. Or say that some unicorns could just stand awkwardly in the background, maybe with their faces hidden behind a tree.

"What have your other classes done?" Sapphire asked. "That would help us think of some ideas."

Once again Twilight was impressed by how comfortable Sapphire was about taking charge. Twilight doubted that Sapphire would have any trouble letting her personality shine. It sparkled naturally.

"I'm not going to tell you!" Professor Sherbet told them. She laughed when the class started grumbling. "I want you all to approach this with fresh eyes. It's the first thing you're going to do together as a class. Have fun with it! Be silly and take chances! I want you all to try your best and get involved. After lunch, brainstorm ideas for the picture, and meet me back in front of the library after the end-of-day bell."

Twilight's heart was pounding so hard, she could feel it in her ears. What was she going to do?

★

The class started talking as soon as Ms. Sherbet trotted away. Everyone seemed to have an idea for the picture and was trying to make their voice heard. Twilight inched back toward the edge of the group, desperate to run away.

"Let's make a unicorn pyramid," Comet called out. "I saw it once at the circus! It was amazing! Okay, someone try to get onto my back!"

But instead of kneeling down, her rose-colored hooves started floating off the ground. Comet had the gift of flight!

"Oh no, not now." Comet groaned. "Could someone pull me down? Just grab my tail."

But the class wasn't listening. Everyone was still trying to get their class picture ideas heard. Twilight might have wanted to hide in the stables, but she could understand what Comet was going through and quickly went over and pulled Comet down by her tail, just as Comet had asked.

"Oof, thank you!" Comet said when she landed firmly on the ground. "That would have been really embarrassing if everyone had been paying attention." She laughed and

stomped her hooves, as if to make sure she was really standing again.

Twilight nodded. She totally got that.

Comet laughed nervously. "I mean, um, I totally have
control over it. It's only sometimes that, well . . . I don't."

Twilight searched for the right words to make Comet
feel better. This was something her sister Sunset was always
good at, joking and making unicorns feel good. Twilight

didn't want to make the same mistake that she had with Shamrock and not say anything at all.

Comet just giggled at the silence. "You're Twilight, right?" she asked. "I'm Comet."

Twilight nodded and squeaked, "I remember."

"Did you like my idea about the unicorn pyramid?" Comet asked.

Twilight thought it would be cool and also very scary. But she worried that saying this would make Comet feel bad. So she just went with a shrug.

"I think it takes a lot of practice and coordination . . . ," Comet said. "And maybe we're not there yet."

Twilight looked over at the squabbling class.

"Did you have any ideas?" Comet asked.

Twilight didn't know how to explain to Comet that she was too scared of this project—and, well, everyone—to even try to think of any ideas.

Comet raised her eyebrows as the silence stretched on. Twilight knew she needed to say *something*, but the more she tried to think of the right thing, the more frozen she felt.

"Okay, well, guess I'd better get back to everyone else," Comet said finally. "Thank you for helping me down. Sorry to ask so many questions. I didn't mean to bother you." Comet quickly trotted over to the group.

Twilight felt her heart sink all the way to her hooves. She'd done it again! Why couldn't she ever think of the right thing to say? Or think of anything to say at all?

Now Twilight didn't feel nervous. She just felt sad.

It felt like all the things she'd worried about were actually happening. She hadn't known the right thing to say all day and had offended the only two classmates she'd talked to! Twilight desperately wanted to go back home. She decided she'd rather disappoint her parents than keep hurting unicorns' feelings.

7

Surprise!

Twilight's heart was heavy when she arrived at the stables, but she was relieved to find the stables empty. Her class was still brainstorming, and everyone else was still out at lunch or exploring the grounds. She thought of all she had seen that day and was sad that she wouldn't get to know the library as she had hoped. But she didn't want to do one more wrong thing. A few hot tears fell down her cheeks as she imagined her parents' disappointed faces.

Twilight quickly spotted stall number twelve. She walked over to her little shelf to start packing her belongings, and found her paint satchel first. The satchel was made of old tan leather and could fold out into an easel. It could

hang comfortably from her neck, and she could take it anywhere she went.

The satchel had belonged to Grandmother Stardust.
When Twilight had been young, her grandmother had trav-

eled the five kingdoms to paint. Grandmother Stardust had given Twilight the satchel full of paints before Twilight started school, saying that her granddaughter was destined to have many great adventures and would need the right tools.

More tears fell down Twilight's face. She would write her grandmother a note and return the paints as soon as she was home.

But before she had a chance to slip the satchel onto her neck, Twilight heard a noise from outside the stall. First it was just hums and gurgles, but then she heard beautiful singing. It was "Somewhere over the Stars," a song she used to sing with her sisters all the time! It felt like a little bit of home had landed in the stables, making her feel suddenly safe. Carefully Twilight snuck out of the stall to investigate. She crept toward the front of the barn, peering into each stall, until she caught a flash of blue.

It was Sapphire! She was swaying inside one of the stalls, her long, braided blue mane swishing in time.

Suddenly Twilight felt like she knew the perfect thing to say. *I'm heading home anyway*, she thought.

Might as well say something before I leave.

"You have the most beautiful voice. It reminds me of stepping into the sunshine," Twilight said almost confidently.

Sapphire stopped singing and sharply spun around to face Twilight. "I thought I was alone!" she screeched.

Twilight felt her stomach drop, as if it were suddenly full of a thousand crystal bricks. She backed away full of regret.

For the first time since her power had appeared, Twilight was happy to feel the familiar tingle of invisibility. She could not disappear fast enough.

"Twilight?" Sapphire asked, her voice squeaking with concern. "Twilight? Where'd you go? I'm sorry I was rude. I just don't usually sing in front of others. And, well, I don't think I'm very good at it. I just like to do it." She dug at the floor with one of her hooves. "But that is the nicest thing anyone has ever said to me. I was just surprised!"

Now *Twilight* was surprised. Sapphire had seemed so very confident.

"Today has been kind of a hard day," Sapphire continued.

Invisible Twilight let out a long breath. *The day has been hard for other unicorns?* she wondered. *I thought it was just me.* "For me too," she admitted quietly, surprising herself.

"Yeah? I have four younger sisters, and I'm used to taking charge . . . ," Sapphire said. "It felt like everyone thought I was really bossy, though."

Twilight was impressed. It made her feel good that Sapphire could tell Twilight something so personal. She wanted to say the right thing to make Sapphire feel better but felt at a loss once more. She let the pause stretch out.

"Oh, okay. I get it." Sapphire sighed. "I'll go now."

Twilight saw that Sapphire's eyes were brimming with tears as she brushed by her.

Twilight did not want to offend another unicorn today. She desperately wanted to help.

"Wait!" Twilight croaked. "I didn't think you were bossy! I've been nervous all day, and you seemed so *confident.* I have two older sisters, and actually, you kind of remind me of them."

Sapphire stopped short. Then her face broke out in a big smile. "Thanks, Twilight."

Twilight remembered that earlier in the day she had thought she and Sapphire were opposites. Now she felt like she understood Sapphire a little more. Well, until she saw Sapphire turning circles in the barn, looking up and down the rows of stalls. Twilight was about to laugh when she realized what Sapphire was looking for.

"Oh, I'm right over here," Twilight called from the hallway outside Sapphire's stall.

Sapphire laughed. "Huh? Where?" she asked. "Are you hiding?"

"I've gone invisible," Twilight said, only a little flustered. Sapphire had been so honest with her that it felt a little easier to be honest back. "Sometimes it happens when I get embarrassed or nervous. I should be reappearing again soon, now that you've noticed. I try to turn visible again myself, but it usually takes someone else realizing that I've disappeared."

Sapphire just nodded. "I guess we were both embarrassed."

Twilight nodded too, before she remembered again that

Sapphire couldn't see that. "Totally," she said. She looked down at her hooves, expecting to see her hooficure appear once more.

But . . . nothing was happening.

Twilight closed her eyes and tried to focus on the sunshine feeling that came with turning visible again. But all she could feel were the cool waves of invisibility.

"Oh no," Twilight whinnied, suddenly very nervous.

"Twilight? What's wrong?" Sapphire asked.

"Um, well . . . I have no idea," Twilight admitted, her voice quivering. "I usually start reappearing again by now."

Sapphire nodded again in understanding. "Don't worry. You'll appear again! You're not the first unicorn at school with this gift. I'm sure there's an explanation!"

Sapphire sounded so sure that it made Twilight's spirits lift a little. But despite all of Sapphire's confidence, Twilight was still invisible, and neither of them had a clue why. She looked over to her stall and saw her half-packed bag. Her stomach sank further.

"That's the thing. I don't think I belong at school,"

Twilight admitted sadly. "Clearly I can't control my power. I always say the wrong thing." Twilight felt lower than she had all day, and tears flooded down her cheeks. She took a deep breath. "I just need to go home."

Sapphire's eyes went wide, and her jaw dropped open in surprise. Then she cocked her head with a big smile. Twilight wiggled, worrying about what Sapphire was going to say.

"But I came in here thinking the same thing!" Sapphire said. "I felt like running home too. I was singing and thinking about packing up my stuff."

Now it was Twilight's eyes that went wide. "But you belong here more than anyone else!" Twilight finally managed.

Sapphire just shook her head, still smiling. "Actually, I think we all belong here. It's only, well, first days are hard. You should totally stay, Twilight."

Twilight blushed happily. Even though her mind had been made up, she felt better hearing Sapphire's words. "You can't even see me, Sapphire," Twilight reminded her. "I mean, think about the class picture. How is my personality supposed to show when you can't even see me?"

Sapphire bit her bottom lip and squinted her eyes a little. "You can't go home when you're invisible, right? That would be super dangerous. I mean, what if you got lost? How would we find you?"

Twilight hadn't even thought about that. "That's true," she said.

"Okay, then," Sapphire went on. "Wait until after the class picture. If you decide you still want to go home, you can tell Ms. Sherbet. But until then, you have to stay here and let me help you become visible."

Twilight thought it over. The plan did make her feel a little better. It would be a lot less embarrassing to figure out the invisibility thing before going to Professor Sherbet.

"Okay, deal," Twilight told her.

"Deal." Sapphire nodded in determination. "We may need some help, though. Let me go get Comet—"

"Did someone say 'COMET'?!"

Sapphire and Twilight looked up to see Comet striking a dramatic pose in the doorway. She flung her mane out and pointed her horn, as if she were posing at a fashion show.

Twilight started to panic. Their last conversation had been such a disaster. What would Comet do when she discovered that Twilight was there too?

"Comet! Great timing," Sapphire told her. "Come over here."

Comet half floated, half trotted over to them. She skidded to a stop in front of Sapphire and almost ran right into invisible Twilight.

"Hi, Comet," Twilight said softly.

"Twilight! Is that you?" Comet exclaimed. "Are you invisible or something?"

"Yeah." Twilight hung her invisible horn. "It's my ability. But I have absolutely no control over it. And, well, now I can't turn back."

"Oh no!" Comet exclaimed. "Ugh. I know that feeling. I was totally lying before—I always need someone to help me down once I start floating. One time I flew all the way to the top of a super-tall tree and couldn't get down. Luckily, my uncle can fly too and got me down."

Twilight's heart swelled. "Actually," she said, "I wanted to tell you about my invisibility problems before, but I just got all tongue-tied. I'm sorry if I made you feel bad."

"Oh, glitterplat!" Comet said, waving her horn. "I was worried that I was bothering you. I feel like I've been bugging everyone all day. I always talk a lot when I get nervous. Or, actually, I talk a lot all the time." Comet paused and laughed.

Twilight was stunned. Both Comet and Sapphire had been nervous too?

"Anyway, I'm super grateful that you helped me down," Comet said. "So, how can *I* help *you*?"

Twilight smiled, despite the fact that she was totally panicked and astonished. It was a weird feeling.

"Glad you asked," Sapphire said. She shook her braided mane and stomped twice. "I think we should go to the library!"

Hope swept through Twilight like a gust of summer wind. Sapphire was right. Surely one of the books in such a calm, sparkling place would have the answer.

"That is the perfect plan!" Comet said.

"I know it is," Sapphire said with a grin.

But Twilight was nervous. She didn't want the whole school to find out she was stuck as an invisible unicorn! "Do you think we could keep this whole invisibility problem a secret?" she asked.

"I love secret missions!" Comet cheered. "But, uh, why does it have to be secret?"

Twilight dug at the wood floors, creating tiny puffs of dust that seemed to appear out of nowhere. "I'm just embarrassed. I don't want everyone to know I'm stuck this way. They'll think I'm some sort of scary ghost."

"I don't think they will, Twilight," Sapphire said. "But we can still keep it a secret. *And* we're going to get you into the class picture, *and* convince you to stay!"

Comet pranced around with excitement. "Brava! Sapphire, you are totally and completely right. Twilight must stay! We all have to! And I will totally help you convince her. And keep it a secret if that's what you want."

Twilight was stunned. For what felt like the billionth time that day, Twilight felt tears well up in her eyes. But this time they were the happy kind. She didn't know if she could really stay at the school forever, but she could at least stay until the end of the day. "Thanks, you guys," she finally said.

"Woo-hoo! Library Secret Mission: Operation Visible," Comet cheered.

8

The Light Idea

The library was filled with students looking at books in the aisles and reading at the large tables in the front. Sapphire, ignoring all the hustle and bustle, marched straight up to Mr. Jazz.

Twilight followed behind. It was difficult to weave her way through all the students when she was invisible. Every time she said "Excuse me," a filly or colt would just look around and then shrug when they didn't see anyone there.

"Mr. Jazz!" Sapphire yelled over the chattering students, waving her horn so he would notice them.

"Hello there!" Mr. Jazz yelled back when he spotted them. Well, when he spotted Comet and Sapphire. "Have you come to pick up your books for the fishing nets? I've added a few more to the pile." Mr. Jazz gestured over to her hook, where about a dozen books now hung.

"No, no. This is much more important," Sapphire said impatiently. "We need some books on unicorn invisibility, please."

"Now, why would you need that?" Mr. Jazz asked.

Twilight froze, and her heart started racing at lightning-bird speed. *Will he figure it out?*

Luckily, Comet was a quick thinker. "Because I've just discovered my magical ability. And I want to learn about other unicorn abilities too," she told him.

Mr. Jazz looked puzzled. Then he shrugged and said, "Well, you're in luck! One of your classmates is already over there with lots of different books about magical abilities. And he has some books on invisibility too."

Comet, Sapphire, and Twilight looked over and saw Shamrock in the corner standing by a table, with books piled all around him. He was peering over his large, black-rimmed glasses, lost in the pages in front of him.

The three fillies thanked Mr. Jazz and walked over to Shamrock. "It's okay," Twilight whispered. "We can tell Shamrock." She had been able to get over her awkwardness with Sapphire and Comet, so maybe she could try again with Shamrock, too.

"Shamrock!" Comet exclaimed loudly. "We super need your help!"

"Uh, Comet, maybe don't say that quite so loudly," Twilight whispered, worried others would hear.

Shamrock whipped his head around so fast that his glasses went askew. "Twilight? Where are you?"

Sapphire rolled her eyes. "She's invisible, as you can't see. That's why we need your help." She used her horn to straighten his glasses for him.

"Oh, okay," Shamrock said.

"She can't turn back," Comet explained further. "And we were hoping one of these books could help. We've got to turn her back before the class picture!"

"Of course," Shamrock agreed. "You can't miss the class picture! The school handbook says—"

"Nope!" Sapphire interrupted him. "This is not about any school rules. This is about showing Twilight she belongs here."

"She wants to go home, and we want her to stay, obviously," Comet explained.

Twilight squirmed uncomfortably. It felt odd having all this attention on her, especially since no one could see her.

Shamrock looked at Sapphire, then at Comet. After a brief pause, he nodded in his serious way.

"Of course you need to stay, Twilight! You're going to help me learn to paint! And if that requires keeping your secret from the teachers, well . . ."

Sapphire, Comet, and Twilight held their breath as they waited for his decision.

"Then we can forget about the handbook!"

Sapphire and Comet whooped and cheered, and Twilight squirmed some more. She had not expected the day to go like this.

"Woo-hoo!" Comet cheered again. "Best first day ever! And I thought the class picture would be my favorite part of the day."

"Oh yeah. What theme did the class decide on?" Sapphire asked.

"No one could agree on anything, so we all just decided to show up with props for different ideas. We can decide right before the picture," Shamrock said, filling them in. "That's why I'm here, actually. I thought we might do something that represents different unicorn magical abilities. Did you know that our powers come from the Four Magical Elements? Every ability is somehow related to water, light, air, or earth."

"I didn't know that," Twilight said. "I guess Comet's flight comes from the air? What about invisibility?"

Shamrock wiggled. He was clearly excited about this question.

"From light, of course," Sapphire told them.

Shamrock nodded enthusiastically. "Exactly!" he said. "And, actually, I think that might be the key to turning Twilight back!"

9

Under the Rainbow

Come on!" Shamrock urged. "Follow me!"

The three fillies followed him out of the library and cantered over to the Looping Lawn. The gnome band had packed up, and the candied apples were nowhere in sight. But the welcome rainbow still hung merrily above their heads.

"Okay," Shamrock said, and they stopped. The four of them panted for a moment, trying to catch their breath. "Sapphire was right: invisibility comes from the magical element of light. And the biggest source of light is sunlight. And here we have a rainbow—"

"And rainbows are refracted light!" Sapphire shouted.

"Uh, guys, what does that mean?" Comet asked.

"It's when a light beam bends as it moves from one thing into another. Like when sunlight goes through air and then hits water," Shamrock explained, sounding very professor-like.

While Comet, Sapphire, and Shamrock went on discussing rainbows and light, Twilight's mind began to wander. She wondered what life would be like if she were invisible forever. She imagined herself living like a ghost in her house, having to knock things over and howl to be noticed. Her heart began to pound, and she tried to take a deep breath to calm down. She liked being quiet, but totally forgotten? That would be the worst.

Twilight noticed Shamrock walking over to a giant water bubble that was spurting out the rainbow sign. She decided she had better pay attention. They were trying to help her, after all.

"So the light from the sun is being refracted through the big raindrop over here," he was saying.

"I'm guessing that a unicorn with a magical water

ability and a unicorn with a magical sunlight ability worked together to create this. Or maybe one unicorn with a magical rainbow ability?" Shamrock wondered aloud.

"Right." Sapphire nodded, clearly trying to get him back on track. "So you're thinking, if Twilight runs through the rainbow here, the refracted light should make her visible again?" Sapphire asked.

"Exactly!" Shamrock yelled. He and Sapphire tapped their horns together in a high-U.

Twilight felt her spirits lift, as if her heart had Comet's gift of flight. "Thank you so much for helping me with this. I was starting to worry that I was going to be invisible forever."

"You totally won't be!" Comet cheered. "We've got this."

Twilight took a deep breath. "Okay. So I just run through the rainbow and I'll reappear, right?"

The other three fillies and colts nodded.

Twilight took another steadying breath and stood a little taller. Even though no one could see her, she wanted to run through this magical rainbow with confidence.

"Okay. Here I go!" Twilight ran back and forth through

the ribbons of colors. She ran through on one side, where the rainbow started and was close to the ground. Then she jumped up so the rainbow would touch her face. Jumping through a rainbow was unlike anything she had done before. It was incredible. She jumped higher than ever, lifted by the possibility of turning back to her old self.

Finally Twilight trotted back toward the group, excited to see the looks on their faces.

10

The Mystery

Twilight still felt the cool waves of invisibility, and looked down to find that her legs had not reappeared. The four unicorns groaned in unison. Jumping through the rainbow hadn't worked.

Twilight's poor stomach had been flipping up and down all day, and now it seemed as if it were somewhere by her invisible hooficured hooves.

If the others could have seen her, they would have seen that Twilight's head hung so low that her horn touched the grass. A few tears fell down her cheeks.

"Thank you so much for trying to help me with this," Twilight told them. "But I don't want to cause you guys any more trouble. You should be getting ready for the class picture! I know you three will think of a great idea for it. I'm just going to go tell Professor Sherbet that it's time for me to go home."

Shamrock looked down bashfully. "You know, I was worried I didn't belong here today either. That's why I kept bringing up the handbook! I thought that if I knew the school rules, then I would know how to be a student. But trying to figure this out has made me realize that Sapphire is right. We all belong here because we can help each other, you know?"

"Yes!" Comet shouted. "I still think this has been the best first day ever. We have this mystery we have to solve together!"

Soon Comet, Sapphire, and Shamrock started shouting silly ideas to solve the "mystery."

Twilight was taken aback and realized . . . they were right. It did feel like she was part of something. She started laughing along with them. "If only I had enough paint to just . . . repaint myself," she said.

Shamrock and Sapphire giggled, but Comet started floating.

"Wait! That gives me an idea." Comet had a huge smile on her face. "Sugar!"

But all she saw were two puzzled looks. Of course, Twilight looked puzzled too, but Comet couldn't see it.

"Uh, Comet, what do you mean by that?" Twilight asked kindly.

"We can cover you in powdered sugar!" she explained.

Twilight had only ever had powdered sugar on candied apples. How could it help a unicorn? But the others looked at each other and nodded seriously.

"Great idea," Shamrock said. "Powdered sugar is sticky enough to stay on."

"True," Sapphire agreed. "I wonder if being able to be seen will bring back your visibility. Like a mind trick or something."

Shamrock nodded his horn. "Brilliant. Only, how do we get all that powdered sugar?" he asked.

"From the kitchens, of course!" Comet told them. "The

campus chefs said that every Friday they make those candied apples that we had this morning at the welcome picnic. So they must have tons of sugar."

"How do you know that, Comet?" Shamrock wondered.

"Because I asked! Those candied apples were the best I've ever had, so I went looking for the recipe. Technically, you're not supposed to go into the kitchen . . . but I consider that more of a suggestion than a rule," Comet told them with an eyebrow wiggle that made them all laugh.

"But don't you think Professor Sherbet will think it's strange when Twilight shows up covered in powdered sugar?" Shamrock asked.

"Not if everyone else is covered in powdered sugar too," Sapphire suggested.

"Huh? Why would that help?" Twilight asked.

"Because it's our class picture idea, of course!" Sapphire told her.

Twilight wasn't as sure as the rest of the group was. Could covering herself in sugar really bring back her visibility? But everyone was excited and happy about the plan,

and she didn't want to spoil it for them. And maybe if they did get the powdered sugar, the class picture wouldn't be so bad. Maybe, just maybe, it might be fun to stand there with these three. She still wasn't sure about the whole school thing, but being part of a group photo of frosted unicorns didn't sound like the worst idea.

"Let's do it," Twilight said.

"Great!" Sapphire was clearly excited. "Shamrock, you go tell the class what's going on. Twilight, you okay with bringing in the other students?"

Twilight's stomach pixies did a few flips. She still didn't like the idea of being the center of attention, but she didn't want to disappoint these magical unicorns who were trying so hard to help her. And that meant they would have to tell the class the plan.

"No problem," Twilight said.

11

Stella and Celest

While Shamrock went to tell the others, Sapphire and Twilight followed Comet to the kitchens. They wove through the Peony Pasture, where some students were still grazing, but no one thought anything of the two first-year fillies walking by.

Finally they reached a large, moss-covered building next to a giant oak tree. The walls of the building were made of stitched bark, and a chimney made of smooth white pebbles twisted out of the rounded roof. Little tufts of gray smoke puffed out.

Comet walked confidently to the front door, which was low and wide and painted the same red as the school barns.

"How many times have you been here?" Sapphire asked.

"Oh, only the one time earlier today. But it was wonderful," Comet told them. She knocked three times with her horn, and the door opened to reveal a small green dragon wearing a bright blue apron.

"Comet! Back again so soon?" The dragon's voice sounded like a million flutes playing in unison. Twilight had never met a dragon before. She was surprised that its voice was so musical. She made a mental note to ask Sunset about this later.

The dragon opened the door wider and moved aside to let them in. The inside was bright, with blue-checkered curtains and cheery yellow walls. Twilight loved it immediately. It reminded her of her home on the farm.

A gray speckled unicorn was using her long horn to stir something in a giant black cauldron in the center of the room. "Don't mind me!" she called. "I have to stir this a hundred times or it will turn to mush. Just a moment!"

"Well, in the meantime, why don't you introduce your friends, Comet?" the dragon asked.

Twilight wiggled with excitement. Had she become visible again? She was so surprised and excited that she almost knocked over a shelf full of spices!

"Wait. *Friends?* How do you know that Comet has brought more than one friend?" Sapphire asked.

Twilight's shoulders sank with disappointment. *Still invisible, I guess. But how does the dragon know I'm here?*

"Ahh, dragons have some magic of their own, little one," the dragon said with a wink.

"One hundred!" the unicorn at the cauldron shouted. "Phew, this recipe is always tricky." She wiped her horn on the checkered cloth hanging on the wall. Her wire-rimmed glasses were still a little foggy from the cauldron's steam. "My name is Celest. And this mysterious dragon is Stella."

"Pleased to meet you all!" Stella said with a nod and a grin.

"Stella, Celest. These are my friends, Sapphire—"

Comet paused to motion toward Sapphire, who waved her horn and said, "Hello!"

"And this . . . ," Comet continued, looking around the room. "Well, actually, Twilight, where are you?"

"Over here by the door," Twilight said. "It's nice to meet you both," she said to Stella and Celest.

"So, we have an invisible filly in our kitchens, huh?" Celest asked.

"We were hoping for some help," Comet told them. "You see, I remembered how you told me about the candied apples recipe, and well . . ."

Suddenly Comet seemed at a loss for words. She looked down at her hooves, as if nervous to ask for such a big favor. Twilight was shocked. She hadn't thought Comet could ever run out of words!

Sapphire started to speak. "Yes, you see, um, we would need, um . . ." Her voice trailed off, as if she couldn't ask them for all that sugar either.

The two unicorns had helped Twilight a lot that day, so she thought it was time she came to their rescue. She took a deep breath and said, "We were wondering if we could take some of your powdered sugar."

"Actually, we'll need a lot of powdered sugar," Sapphire said, finding her voice. "Enough to cover our whole class with it."

They were all silent for a moment. Then Stella and Celest burst out laughing.

"I'm guessing this has something to do with class pictures?" Celest finally said, once she had recovered.

The three fillies nodded.

Celest tapped her hoof on the ground, and Stella

scratched her scaly head with one long, purple-painted claw. Then they looked at each other for a long time, as if chatting silently. Twilight wondered if that was actually what they were doing.

"Okay, here's what we can do," Stella finally told them. "You can have one bag. We need the sugar for our recipes, and I think it would be a waste to just dump all of it out. But we can spare one bag, and it should cover one unicorn filly, which is all you really need, anyway. Right?"

"Well, actually—" Comet started to say, but Sapphire interrupted.

"Deal," she said.

"All right, but you have to make us a promise," Celest said.

Twilight bit her lip. What kind of bargain would they have to make?

"You have to send us a copy of the picture!" Stella said. She and Celest burst out laughing again.

The fillies joined in with them. It was a silly plan, after all. Twilight might have been just an invisible unicorn with an odd plan, but, she suddenly realized, she had made some wonderful friends on this strange day. And with that thought, she wondered if going home was quite the right thing to do after all.

★

The three fillies borrowed some rope from Celest and Stella before they left the kitchen. By tying the rope to the bag and then around their waists, Sapphire and Comet were able to drag the large bag of powdered sugar behind them. Twilight wanted to help, but everyone agreed that a rope hanging in midair would cause suspicion.

On the way back, Twilight smiled as she listened to her new friends laugh and chat. Unicorn U didn't feel scary anymore. It was actually really fun. And Twilight couldn't stop thinking about how she wanted to be a student here after all.

But then Twilight remembered she was still invisible. What if she was like this forever? Would the school even allow her to stay? Her heart pounded at the thought.

"We're almost there, guys," Sapphire said, interrupting Twilight's spiral of worries. "Operation Visible is almost complete."

Twilight smiled. "Thank you for all your help, you guys. This day has been way better than I thought it would be. And I really want to stay here at Unicorn U."

Comet and Sapphire whooped and cheered. They bounced so much that some powdered sugar escaped in little sparkly puffs.

"But I don't think they'll let an invisible filly hang around . . . ," Twilight admitted when they'd calmed down. A few invisible tears fell down her invisible checks.

"It's going to be okay, Twilight," Sapphire said, still as confident as ever. "If the sugary mind trick doesn't work, then we'll just tell Professor Sherbet. She'll know what to do."

"You're not going anywhere, Twilight!" Comet said.

They met up with Shamrock, who was pacing back and forth under the rainbow banner.

"Shamrock!" Comet called out to him.

Twilight could see a look of relief fall over his face when he saw them. Then he saw at the bag of powdered sugar, and his face scrunched up again. "You guys! I thought you were going to get enough sugar for everyone?"

"Well, turns out that's a lot of sugar, and Stella and Celest couldn't part with all of it," Comet told him with a shrug.

The group paused. Twilight realized that the three fillies had just been happy with the experience of getting the sugar. They hadn't even thought of how this would affect the over-all plan. Twilight, of course, started to panic.

"Oh, don't worry. I have a way better plan!" Sapphire said.

12

Sugar Time

Okay. You ready, Twilight?" Comet yelled from the top of the hill.

Twilight waited at the bottom of the hill next to the blueberry bush, just as they had planned. She breathed in and out slowly, preparing herself for the next step. "Ready!" she called back.

Comet ran down the hill, and then—suddenly—a rose-colored blur flew right over Twilight, showering her in sparkling powdered sugar. Twilight giggled as the sugary sweetness covered her completely.

"Oof!" Comet landed just beyond her with a hard thud. "Did you see that?" she bellowed. "I totally made that

landing! That was the coolest! Should we do it again?"

Twilight chuckled. "You're fearless!"

Sapphire and Shamrock came cantering down the hill, whooping and hollering with glee. Just as they reached the sugary mess at the bottom of the hill, a loud bell rang out, followed by a chorus of birds chirping, "End of class! End of class!"

Sapphire laughed. "Professor Sherbet was right. You really can't miss that bell. Hurry, guys. We still have to finish getting ready for the picture!"

★

The class assembled on the library's front steps. Shamrock had done a good job spreading the word about the change in plans.

Ms. Sherbet came galloping over to them, neighing in her joyful, merry way. "Well, everyone! I think this is the most impressive class picture I've ever seen. You guys have really done something unique."

The class giggled together and shared secretive looks.

"Can you guess the theme, Professor?" Sapphire asked.

"Well, hmm . . ." Professor Sherbet thought for a minute before shaking her head. "I have to admit, I have no idea! Will you tell me?"

"We're in disguise!" Comet yelled.

"We call this the Mystery Picture," Twilight explained, smiling wide. She was so happy, she could burst. She felt like a totally different unicorn from the one who'd played the name game earlier that day.

Professor Sherbet neighed merrily again. "Wonderful! Wonderful!"

Twilight looked around at her fellow classmates. "Mystery Picture" described the scene perfectly. Everyone had covered themselves head to toe with something different. Comet had flown up to pull down the branches of a newly blooming tree and covered herself with bright yellow pollen. She looked like a ray of sunshine. Shamrock was dressed as a gnome. He'd used a red blanket for a cape and had found a red cap that a gnome had left behind, and he'd topped it off with a fake beard. Sapphire had woven a blanket out of vines and leaves and thrown it over herself. She'd copied one of the easier designs from a library book. And all the other classmates had creatively disguised themselves as well. Despite being hidden, it still felt like everyone's personalities shone through. It was the coolest.

After the picture, Ms. Sherbet told them it was time for dinner and then it was off to bed. Comet, Sapphire, and Shamrock tossed off their disguises and trotted away in the direction of the Looping Lawn.

Twilight watched them leave. She felt frozen. She couldn't toss her disguise off so easily. If she washed off the powdered sugar, she would be invisible again.

There was nothing left to do. It was time to talk to Professor Sherbet. Twilight would tell her all about the invisibility, but after the day she'd had, Twilight knew she belonged at Unicorn U with her friends. Thinking about everything that had happened made her feel like she was drinking a cup of cocoa with extra marshmallows and whipped cream. She just had to tell Ms. Sherbet the truth. The professor would understand. Twilight wiggled and wiggled and let the powdered sugar fall off.

"Twilight! Twilight!" Sapphire called over.

Twilight looked up and saw that Sapphire, Comet, and Shamrock were looking over at her, waiting for her to join them. *But wait,* Twilight thought. *They're looking right at me. How do they know where to look?*

Twilight looked down and started jumping for joy. She could see her purple-painted hooves shining through the left-over powdered sugar! And her jet-black coat, too! Twilight couldn't stop laughing and dancing.

"Whoa! Why so excited?" asked the unicorn who'd taken the class picture.

Normally Twilight would be embarrassed and would fade out. But she was so happy that she didn't care who saw her crazy dance moves.

"I think I can finally see myself," she told him. Then she had an exciting idea. "Hey, would you mind taking another picture? One of me and my friends?"

"Sure can!" the photographer agreed.

★

A week later Twilight added one more thing to stall number twelve. It was a wooden frame that held the photo of her with Shamrock, Comet, and Sapphire. The four unicorn fillies and colts smiled broadly, powdered sugar smudged on all their faces.

Twilight took a step back to admire the scene. *I'm so lucky to have friends like these,* she thought. *I can't wait for all the adventures to come!*

Sapphire's
Special Power

1

The Royal Messenger

Sapphire was so excited that she couldn't stop moving. It felt like her hooves were filled with dancing beans. She dashed among her fellow first years of Unicorn University, making sure everyone was ready to go. They were all gathered together on the Looping Lawn, under the two tallest oak trees. The large knobbly branches stretched out far above them, covering the rainbow cluster of unicorn students.

Sapphire noticed that the sun was lower in the sky. She straightened her shoulders and shook her long, braided blue mane. "Okay!" she shouted to get everyone's attention. "Let's get into our places. Shamrock, Firefly, you guys head across the field to make sure the banner is high enough so that Fairy Green can see it when she flies in."

Shamrock, a mint-green colt and one of Sapphire's closest friends, nodded so enthusiastically that his large, black-rimmed glasses went crooked. Using her horn, Sapphire straightened them for him and then held out a large conch shell on a string. "I borrowed this from gym class. Just yell into it, and we'll be able to hear you from across the lawn." Shamrock slipped his horn through the string and straightened his neck so that the string fell down around his shoulders.

"Wow, cool, just like Coach Ruby!" said Firefly, a red-and-gold unicorn.

Sapphire watched Shamrock and Firefly run across the field. She still couldn't believe they were all going to meet a real fairy tomorrow. Fairies lived throughout the five kingdoms, but as royal messengers they usually only appeared to deliver important notes or news. So you didn't meet them unless you were someone super important. But when Sapphire's teacher, Professor Sherbet, had heard that her close friend Fairy Green was traveling through Sunshine

Springs for the annual Fairy Gathering, the professor had asked if her friend could stop by to talk to the first-year students.

Ever since she was little, Sapphire had wanted to travel the five kingdoms. Growing up by the ocean, she'd seen ships travel by from all over the world. She would spend hours at her bedroom window, wondering where they were going and why. But the ships were always just out of reach, close enough to dream about but too far away for Sapphire to talk to anyone on board. So she couldn't help but feel like this meeting with Fairy Green was the start of something very big. As her good friend Twilight would say, it felt like pixies were dancing in her stomach.

It was time for stage two of the Welcome Plan. Sapphire turned to a snow-white unicorn with a red-and-white striped mane named Peppermint, and to a three-legged gray unicorn named Storm. "Okay. Is the banner ready?" Sapphire asked.

The banner certainly looked ready. Sapphire marveled at how Peppermint and Storm had managed to arrange the flowers so that they spelled out WELCOME TO UU, FAIRY

GREEN! They used bright flowers for the letters and green plants for the background. Sapphire noticed that all the flowers had the same shimmer. Curious, she leaned in closer.

"I used my ability with weather to make it shine like that," Storm said proudly. "I protected the morning dew so it wouldn't dry up with the sun."

"Great work, Storm," Sapphire said with a nod of approval.

Peppermint scoffed and flipped her mane. "Well, I used my weaving ability to knit the flowers all together. We wouldn't even have a banner without me," she whined.

"Oh, it's really glitter-tastic! You guys make a fantastic team!" Comet assured her. Sapphire nudged her rose-colored friend with her flank. Comet was always so positive and encouraging. She always made everyone feel like they were part of things, like they belonged. Sapphire loved that about Comet.

"It's absolutely perfect," Sapphire agreed.

Peppermint and Storm grinned and tapped their horns together in a high-U.

"Okay, Comet," Sapphire said. "You're up next!"

Comet had woven fairy's thread through her mane, and it glittered in the bright afternoon sun. But despite all the sparkle, Comet suddenly seemed rather dull. Her eyebrows were scrunched and her mouth twisted to the side. It was a look that was certainly unusual for cheerful Comet.

"What's wrong?" Sapphire asked, her own eyebrows arching with concern.

Comet hoofed the grass beneath her. "It's just, well, I'm nervous about my part. I'm sure I can fly up to the top of the trees, no problem, and I bet I can manage to tie the ropes to the trees. Just . . . what if I can't get back down again?"

Comet had the gift of flight, but she was still learning and had a hard time with her landings. She almost never made it back down without a teacher to help. But they had all agreed to enact the Welcome Plan on their own, no grown-ups allowed.

Sapphire smiled at her sparkly friend. She knew just what to do.

"Peppermint!" Sapphire called—perhaps a little too loudly. Peppermint was right next to her, after all. "Could you weave some ivy around Comet?"

"Um, totes. That's so easy," Peppermint said with her signature mane flip. The red-and-white strands of her mane twisted and twirled together like a bunch of little candy canes. Sapphire couldn't help but admire it.

"Great," Sapphire said. "How about you wrap ivy around Comet's waist, and leave a lot of extra so I can hold one end while Comet flies up to the trees. Then, Comet, when you're ready, we'll just pull you back down again!"

A huge smile with bright pink dimples immediately replaced Comet's frown. "Let's do this!" she cheered.

"Woo-hoo!" Sapphire joined in, followed by enthusiastic whoops from Peppermint and Storm.

Before long the beautiful banner was hung between the oak trees. After finding the right height, Shamrock and Firefly ran over to the group.

The unicorns admired their work. Sapphire was proud of her classmates for pulling it all off. She thought about her own first day at Unicorn University and the rainbow banner that had welcomed the first year students. She wanted to make sure Fairy Green felt just as welcome.

"And now for the final step," Sapphire said. "Twilight, do you have the Spotlight Flowers?"

Twilight was another one of Sapphire's best friends, and she had the gift of invisibility. Spotlight Flowers were found only in one patch of field on campus, and from afar you could see their giant heads lifting up and casting beams of different-colored lights. Students loved to go up to the Magic Meadow to watch the Spotlight Flowers in the evening, as the flowers seemed to respond to each other and it was like watching lights dance. But whenever anyone got close, the flowers would curl up and disguise themselves as weeds, making it impossible to tell which was the disguised Spotlight Flower and which was a regular old weed.

That was, until Sapphire and Comet had hatched a plan. It had taken some convincing to get Twilight and Shamrock on board, but eventually they'd figured out that Twilight's invisibility allowed her to sneak into the fields so that the flowers wouldn't know a thing. When Sapphire had dreamt up the welcome banner, she'd known just how to make sure Fairy Green would see the banner even if she flew in at night. The Spotlight Flowers would make the perfect royal welcome. Luckily, Twilight had agreed to gather a basketful of the special plants to replant under the big oak trees.

But looking around now, Sapphire couldn't see Twilight anywhere. *Oh no*, Sapphire worried. *Is Twilight stuck invisible again?*

2

Bright Lights, Big Banner

Sapphire looked to the stables and was relieved to see Twilight galloping toward the group, but when Twilight got closer, Sapphire could see tears brimming in Twilight's eyes, and her lower lip trembling with worry. "Saph, I can't find the basket anywhere," she said when she stopped short, still panting from the quick pace. "I picked the flowers right after breakfast, but I have no idea where the basket went between then and now!"

A chorus of groans came from the students. Sapphire knew that Twilight hated attention more than anything else, and Twilight's hooves were shimmering in and out of invisibility, which usually meant she was panicking. Sapphire

needed to get everyone to focus elsewhere. And fast.

She jumped into action. "It's okay, guys! We just need to retrace our steps. Who remembers seeing the basket after Twilight came out of the Spotlight Garden?" Sapphire asked.

The whole class erupted like a volcano with thoughts and ideas of where the basket could be. But absolutely no one was listening to the others. It reminded Sapphire of their first day of school, when they'd all been trying to think of a class picture idea.

Then Shamrock blurted out, "The Crystal Library!"

At first Sapphire just thought he meant they should go to the library to figure out the problem. As much as Sapphire loved that magical place, she didn't think the answer was going to be in a book. But when she turned to Shamrock to tell him so, she saw a look in his eyes that she'd never seen before. It was a bit like when he was trying to figure out the answer to a tough question, like he was looking far into the distance. But this look was way more intense. Like he was seeing light-years ahead.

Then Shamrock yelled, "The Peony Pasture!"

That made the whole class pay attention. In fact, everyone stopped talking at once. Shamrock was usually a very calm unicorn, certainly not one to just shout stuff.

Just as suddenly as it had come, Shamrock seemed to jump out of his trance. His face broke into a big, goofy smile that pushed his glasses up to his eyebrows. "Follow me," he told the group in his usual voice. "I know where the flowers are!" And he dashed off in the direction of the Silver Lining Stables, the students' dormitories. The class hurried after him, many asking what had happened, but Shamrock ignored them all.

Shamrock stopped short in front of Twilight's stall, and Sapphire arrived not long after him. She smiled at the photo that always hung below the shiny golden number twelve.

The picture was from their very first day of school, with Sapphire, Comet, Shamrock, and Twilight all posed happily with powdered sugar smudged all over their faces. Sapphire had been so nervous that first day. It had felt like she would never belong. But now, only one month in, she couldn't imagine being anywhere else. She loved everything about Unicorn U.

With Twilight's permission, Shamrock swung open Twilight's door to reveal a basket full of Spotlight Flowers.

"Of course!" Twilight squeaked. "We stopped by here to get some string for the banner, and I must have left the basket behind. Thank you, Shamrock!"

"But how'd you know that?" Storm asked. "Only Twilight and I came by here. Weren't you still out on the lawn?"

"I think I've developed my ability," Shamrock told them, his eyes sparkling with joy. "I think I have a special photographic memory! All of a sudden, I could rewind my day like a—" He stopped short and squinted a little, as if searching for the right word. "Like a memory movie! And I remembered that you had the basket in the Crystal Library but not in the Peony Pasture at lunch, but you did have the string. So it made sense that you would have left the flowers when you got your art supplies from your stall!" he finished happily, and slightly out of breath.

The class cheered and started back up to the giant oak trees, Spotlight Flowers in hand. Sapphire nudged Shamrock on the way, and he looked back at her with a grin. She could tell how happy he was that his special power had finally appeared. And she was happy for her friend.

Once they reached the banner, Sapphire stood back and directed everyone to carefully replant the flowers and, using Twilight's string, aim them to light up the banner with soft blues, pinks, and yellows. It was spectacular.

The dinner bell rang, and Sapphire watched her classmates dash off to the Peony Pasture for apples and oats before bed. But she hung back just a bit to admire their creation one more time. Butterflies danced in her stomach, and she couldn't help but smile with excitement. She was going to meet a fairy tomorrow!

3

Breakfast Dreams

The next morning, Sapphire opened her eyes in time to watch the sun rise from her stall window. The stable was quiet—everyone was surely still sleeping—but Sapphire couldn't go back to sleep. The dancing beans in her hooves were back in full force. The day was finally here! Sapphire crept softy out of her stall, careful not to let the door bang and wake up the other fillies. The seaweed wreath her sisters had sent from home swung quietly as she slowly let the door close behind her. Avoiding all the creaky planks, she made her way out to the fields. The sun was still low in the sky, and the whole campus was bathed in a warm orange and pink light. It felt like a different world, making the morning even more exciting.

When she was far enough away from the stables, Sapphire broke into a quick canter. She raced across the Looping Lawn, the fresh morning dew brushing her blue calves as she ran through the grass. She smiled with delight when she reached their beautiful banner hanging between the oak trees. She felt so proud of their work as she watched the Spotlight Flowers' early-morning light show. Folding her four legs beneath her, she sat down and looked out across the campus. She could see the red barns of the Silver Lining Stables, looking as asleep as its dwellers, and the Crystal Library, the castle-like structure glittering even though the sun was so low.

The view was beautiful, and she was just so comfortable. Right before sleep overtook her, Sapphire saw a green blur in the sky overhead stop short. *Could it be?* Sapphire wondered. *Did I just see Fairy Green? Or am I already dreaming?*

★

Sapphire woke with a start. The sun was now high in the sky, and she could feel that the campus had come alive, the voices of her classmates chattering in the distance. *Have I missed the morning bell?* She quickly got to her hooves, blinking the sleep out of her eyes. Her belly rumbled as she cantered over to the Peony Pasture, hoping to make it in time for breakfast.

She was happy to see her classmates still clustered around their favorite apple tree. She didn't know why they chose it every day, but it was the first place where they had all eaten, and somehow they had silently agreed to gather there ever since.

Sapphire wedged herself between Comet and Twilight and plucked a big, pink apple from the branch above her. She tried to catch up with the morning conversation as she munched.

"I actually developed my ability when I was sleeping," Peppermint was saying. "I had fallen asleep by the fire after I'd been up late reading. I woke with my mother's knitting all stitched around me. I guess sleeping me had wanted a blanket."

Sapphire laughed with the rest of her class, imagining the sight.

But the laughter stopped quickly when a group of older unicorns came up to them. Older unicorns almost never talked to first years. Sapphire gulped the mouthful of apple she'd been chewing and exchanged a questioning look with Comet. Sapphire noticed the other first years were fidgeting around her. Clearly everyone was nervous!

"We just wanted to congratulate you guys on that welcome banner for Fairy Green," said Flash, a hot-pink unicorn with a rainbow mane. Sapphire couldn't believe the captain of the senior hoofball team and basically the coolest unicorn ever was congratulating them on her idea. She could feel her cheeks heat up.

Peppermint tossed her mane with an especially dramatic flair and said, "*I* wove the flowers together. I was just telling everyone about my special abilities."

"And I added the glittering dew," Storm offered.

"And Twilight gathered the Spotlight Flowers because she can turn invisible, and Shamrock found the flowers because of his photographic memory!" Comet added, hovering above the grass a little in her excitement.

"But it wouldn't have been possible without Comet! She flew up and hung the banner for us," Shamrock added.

"And Sapphire—" Twilight started, but she was too quiet for others to hear her.

Flash had started talking again. "Sounds like you guys are the dream team. Your abilities are awesome."

Flash's silver-haired teammate, Chrome, said, "Yeah. You guys are totally the coolest first years that Unicorn U has ever seen. Our biggest project was trying to figure out what ability Headmaster Starblaze had. Definitely not as awesome."

"Oh yeah!" Flash remembered. "Must be something super top secret if no one has discovered it yet."

"You mean you never figured it out?" Shamrock asked.

"Nope," said Chrome. "But hey, if anyone can figure it out, it's you guys."

With that, Chrome and Flash headed out, leaving the first-year students in a happy glow.

Sapphire just shrugged and turned back to her breakfast. Why were they talking about the boring old headmaster when they could have been talking about the royal messenger who was eating with their teachers *right now*? Sapphire looked over to see a small green figure sitting on one of the low branches at the teachers' tree. The fairy and Professor Sherbet were leaning in close together, laughing hysterically. Sapphire wondered what they were talking about. Could it be one of their adventures? Sapphire imagined herself sitting at the teachers' tree, all grown up and laughing about her own explorations. "And that's what happens when you mistake a mermaid for a sea serpent!" she imagined herself saying, to a chorus of laughter.

"Hey, Saph," Twilight said, drawing her friend back to the present.

Sapphire shook herself loose from the daydream. "Yeah, Twilight?"

"Did you forget your notebook? I can go back to the stables with you. I have to get my paints, anyway."

"Twilight, you genius!" Sapphire hung her long neck around Twilight in a hug. She was happy her friend had reminded her of her brand-new notebook. Sapphire had asked her mom to send it to her when she'd found out that Fairy Green was coming. She wanted to record everything the fairy said. This was the start of Sapphire's dreams coming true!

4

Meeting Ms. Green

After getting Sapphire's notebook and Twilight's paints, the two unicorns hurried to the Magic Meadow to meet up with their class. The Meadow was farther out on campus and was used a lot less than other spaces, but Sapphire thought it was one of the most beautiful places at Unicorn U.

When they arrived, Twilight and Sapphire could see that the rest of the class had already gathered under the large weeping willow. It's long, delicate branches and dark green leaves hung around the students like curtains. Some branches extended over the stream bank, and some dipped into the glittering water. Everyone was clustered around

Professor Sherbet, who stood next to a tall tree stump. When Twilight and Sapphire joined the group, they could see that Fairy Green was perched atop the stump, which allowed her to look at them at eye level. Her wings were made of what appeared to be large, green leaves, and her hair was piled high atop her head in a swirl that reminded Sapphire of the drippy sandcastles she would build at the beach. Fairy Green's face and hands were forest green, and her dress was made of different types of moss, all woven together in

a striped pattern. *Fairy Green looks like she's part of the meadow*, Sapphire thought.

"Hello, students!" Professor Sherbet called out in her usual warm and friendly way. Today the professor wore a crown made of moss that looked just like the moss of Fairy Green's dress. "I am so excited to introduce you all to my very good friend, the one and only Fairy Green! Please gather round while she tells us some things about her life, and later we can ask her some questions."

Fairy Green flew smoothly from her perch and hovered in front of the students. Now she was slightly above them, making the very air her stage. "Thank you, my friend," she said, turning to Professor Sherbet. It was clear the two had known each other for a long time. Sapphire hoped she would stay friends with Twilight, Comet, and Shamrock for just as long. "And thank you, students, for the wonderful banner! I've been all over the world, but I've never felt so welcome." She paused to smile at them all. Sapphire could feel her heart swell with pride.

"I'm on my way to the annual Fairy Gathering," Fairy

Green continued. Her voice was much louder than one would expect, given her size. She was as loud as any unicorn, or even a dragon. "It is my favorite time of the year, for it is when fairies throughout the five kingdoms come together in our Woodland City to meet to discuss the world's news. There are parties and so much music! It is the true meaning of magic." Her forest-green eyes lit up when she spoke. "There are lots of different types of fairies with different types of magic. We may seem very different from you but unicorns and fairies have something very important in common. Does anyone know what that is?" She let the question hang in the air as the first years struggled to figure out what she meant.

Sapphire's heart soared as she raised her horn. She knew just what Fairy Green meant.

"Yes, you with the magnificent blue coat," Fairy Green called out.

"Hello, Fairy Green. My name is Sapphire," she said in a loud, clear voice. "Like unicorns, fairies draw their magic from the Four Magical Elements."

Professor Sherbet neighed merrily, clearly proud of her pupil.

Fairy Green clapped her hands together softly, filling the air with the sound of rustling leaves. "Very good, Sapphire!"

Sapphire felt as if she were floating on the ocean, buoyed up by happiness. This was the best day of her life.

"All fairies draw their strength from one of the Four Magical Elements: light, water, earth, and air. As a Forest Fairy, I am most connected to the earth element. But I do have wings, and while they are not as strong as the Flight Fairies' wings, I am connected to the air as well. Just as you unicorns, no matter where your ability comes from, are connected to all four elements too." Fairy Green paused again to let the words sink in.

"Both unicorns and fairies come from Sunshine Springs," she continued. "And so we all share a very special connection and friendship, one that goes back thousands and thousands of years. Does anyone know this story?"

This time it was Shamrock's turn to wave his horn in the air. He was so enthusiastic that it was surprising he managed to keep his glasses on straight. Fairy Green gestured for him to answer.

"I have read only a little about this," Shamrock began, "but I think it has something to do with your basket of fairy dust? Unicorns and fairies found it together."

Sapphire nodded as he spoke. She and Shamrock had been doing some research and they had read this in one of the books the librarian, Professor Jazz had recommended.

"Your unicorns are very quick, Professor Sherbet!" Fairy Green turned to her friend with a smile. "I see great things for your class."

Professor Sherbet beamed.

"Quite right, Shamrock," Fairy Green said. "Long ago, fairies and unicorns sent out an expedition team to map all of Sunshine Springs, and this team found the Sacred Forest. You see, at one time all the fairies lived in different parts of our kingdom, not in the four sacred cities as we do today, and together they found the Tree of Knowledge. Legend has it that the pollen swirled and covered the team completely. It looked as if powdered sugar had rained from the heavens."

Fairy Green gave them all a little wink. Clearly Professor Sherbet had told her the story of their class picture.

Sapphire looked over to Twilight, who was blushing but still had a big smile on her face. The rest of the class was laughing along.

"The pollen made the unicorns sneeze, but to the fairies it was magic. We learned that it would make us stronger. And would allow us to travel far distances without wearing out our wings. I can't tell you how, as we fairies have *some* secrets, but it is only with this basket that I am able to travel the five kingdoms. You may know this pollen as fairy dust." She flew back to her stump to pick up her basket. It was made of a deep brown bark with a lid that fit perfectly, and a long strap made of woven ivy that allowed her to carry it over her shoulder. Putting the basket down, she resumed her story. "The unicorns helped us build our city around the tree, which would become the Woodland City and our capital. In return, the fairies brought builders from throughout the five kingdoms and helped create libraries, like your Crystal Library, all over Sunshine Springs. The unicorns wanted to record all that they learn from us, and from all the other creatures of the five kingdoms for generations to come."

The students started chattering immediately after Fairy Green had stopped speaking. They'd had no idea that this was where the libraries had come from. Sapphire couldn't wait to discuss it with Professor Jazz, later.

"Okay. I think it's about time for questions!" Fairy Green said, and she was met with an immediate wave of horns. The first years wiggled and jumped to be called on, looking like a rainbow flag waving together. Sapphire thought about all the questions she wanted to ask. Comet was called on first, probably because she had hovered so high in her excitement that Shamrock had to pull her down by her tail. "Is 'Fairy Green' your real name? It seems sorta plain for you, if you don't mind me saying."

Fairy Green chuckled, and Sapphire thought it sounded just like a swirl of leaves whipping together in the wind. "Very good question. No, 'Fairy Green' is not my full name. It's the name I use when traveling. My real name is known

by all fairies, but I share it with only very few other creatures, for it holds great power. Does anyone else have a
question?"

Fairy Green answered all their questions, from "Where
do fairies sleep?" (in hammocks) to "What is your favorite
kingdom to visit?" (Soaring Spires) to "Do you ever travel
by bird?" (She did when she was too young use fairy dust).

Sapphire was swept away by it all, making mental notes
to record later in her notebook. Her mouth hung slightly open,
and she only noticed that a little bit of drool had escaped
when she was called on for
the last question.

"I believe the final
question should go to
Sapphire, since she answered
my first question. And I do
love symmetry," Fairy Green
said smartly.

"You said that you have

to use fairy dust to travel the five kingdoms. Does everyone have to have something magical in order to explore?" Sapphire felt good about this question. She'd have to know what she'd need to be an explorer, and she truthfully didn't know where to start.

"You know, no one has ever asked me that before," Fairy Green told her. Then she paused for much longer than she had for the other questions. "Yes," she said finally. "I do believe all creatures who travel widely must possess a certain type of magic."

"Like a magical ability?" Peppermint asked.

"Yes, I suppose so. Something like that," Fairy Green answered.

Those words hit Sapphire like a bag of crystal bricks.

But I don't have a magical ability, she thought.

Professor Sherbet thanked Fairy Green and dismissed the first years to their break, but Sapphire couldn't hear any of it. It felt like pixies were buzzing in her ears, repeating what Fairy Green had said. *There can never be any explor-*

ing for me, thought Sapphire. Tears welled up and threatened to fall.

Out of the corner of her eye, she saw Comet, Twilight, and Shamrock move toward her with sad looks on the faces, but Sapphire just shook her head and walked farther into the meadow.

5

Taking Flight

Sapphire decided to run. She ran as fast as she could through the low stream, feeling the cool water splash around her hooves. It cleared her head, and soon enough she had a thought.

I just have to find my magic.

Sapphire stopped abruptly, causing the water to form a wave big enough to splash onto her chest, cooling her off. After stepping out of the stream and shaking the water off her flanks, Sapphire headed up the grassy bank. She thought all about what Fairy Green had said, and how fairies had not had the magic to travel before they'd found the special pollen. After that, they'd been able to go anywhere. Even her friends hadn't had magic before they'd discovered their abilities. What if Sapphire had simply not found her ability yet? After all, she'd never cared to search for one before. Perhaps she just had to give her ability an extra push. Then she'd have the magic she needed to reach her dreams.

Using her horn, Sapphire pulled her new notebook from the bag that hung around her shoulders, and laid the book out in front of her. *This will be called my quest book*, she thought. Then she took out the little inkwell. The notebook was plain, just made of a simple bark, but the inkwell was

spectacular. It was made from an extra large pearl that had been hollowed out. Sapphire pulled the cork stopper out with her teeth before dipping her horn into the bright blue ink. It was a little awkward, writing without a desk, but she decided to go for it anyway.

Very carefully Sapphire wrote "The Magic Quest" at the top of the page. But then she paused. *Where do I start?* she wondered.

Sapphire's mother could breathe underwater by asking air bubbles to come together to create a sort of helmet around her. She harvested seaweed, and this ability with air was very helpful. Sapphire wondered if she had some sort of air gift as well. Maybe she could even fly! That would be the perfect way to explore. She could simply fly to all the five kingdoms, like a fairy! Sapphire decided to find Comet to see if her flying friend could help her unlock this ability.

Sapphire was so excited to have a plan that she felt like singing. She dipped her horn into the ink once again and, under the title, wrote "Learn to fly."

After packing up her bag again, Sapphire skipped to the Friendly Fields. Luckily, she and Comet had hoofball practice together, so it was perfect timing.

Coach Ruby was blowing her final huddle-up whistle as Sapphire joined the group. She and Comet were on the junior hoofball team, made up of first and second years.

In the spring they would play junior hoofball teams from other schools in Sunshine Springs. Sapphire had joined the team because she loved playing with her sisters and cousins at home, and she was usually the MVU (Most Valuable Unicorn) when they played over the holidays. Comet had decided to join the team too because she thought it would be fun to run around all day. Plus, she liked the uniforms.

Sapphire saw Flash directing the senior hoofball team on the other side of the arena, in complicated plays Sapphire didn't recognize. The junior team was still learning the basics.

"Pair up, everyone," Coach Ruby said. "I want you all to find your hoofball strengths this week. We'll be doing some practice games next week, and you all should figure out which positions you'd like to try. If you love to kick, and can kick in the right direction, think about being a forward. If you like the horn toss, think about being goalie. If you love to run, think about defense. And if you have questions, ask." Coach Ruby blew her conch shell horn once in dismissal. Sapphire liked Coach Ruby. She always got to the point quickly.

Sapphire and Comet walked away from the group and started passing the hoofball back and forth, warming up.

"Comet," Sapphire said, trapping the ball underneath her front right hoof. "What do you think about figuring out our strengths a little differently today?"

Recognizing Sapphire's "adventure voice," Comet cheered, "Oh yeah!" And then she said a little more softly, "What do you mean, though?"

"Okay. You know I want to be an explorer more than anything else, right?" Sapphire asked.

Comet nodded. "Of course!"

"Right," Sapphire said. "But Fairy Green said I'd need magic."

"Yeah, but, Saph—" Comet started to argue.

Sapphire just shook her head and kept going, "Well, I think I just haven't developed my magical ability yet. And it needs a little push, you know?"

"Totally makes sense," Comet said. "I mean, it's not like I started flying randomly. I was baking with my aunt one day, and my oat doughnuts were always getting messed up. Like, I could not figure out how to get the holes round enough so that I could serve them with my horn. Sure, they tasted okay. But I wanted to be able to slip them off my horn onto a plate like the real chefs do."

"Yes . . . ," Sapphire said impatiently, motioning with her horn for Comet to get to the point.

"Right, right," Comet went on. "Well, my whole huge family was over—like, everyone—and it was after dinner and I had put the doughnuts into the oven to be ready for dessert. So I pull them out, and there they are, super round!

Not wanting to mess it up, more calm than I'll, like, ever be again, I slipped them onto my horn and carried them out to the table in the garden. With a perfect flourish I slipped all the doughnuts onto the table, just like a chef! Well, I got so excited, I felt lighter than air. And I just started flying and flying. And that's when I got stuck in a tree. And then my uncle flew up—he has the flight gift too—and got me back down again. But anyway, it was when I was super excited. So, why don't you try thinking about your favorite things?"

So it was all about feeling lighter than air. That made sense to Sapphire. She closed her eyes and took a breath, like Twilight did when she needed to calm herself. Actually, Sapphire was pretty sure that Shamrock had taught her that trick, because he used it when he started going off on a long explanation.

"This is a great idea, Comet. My favorite things. . . . Water and swimming, learning about the five kingdoms, reading," Sapphire started. She felt happy thinking about everything she loved, but not lighter.

"Maybe more specific?" Comet offered.

"What do you mean?" Sapphire asked.

"Think like Twilight. Details," Comet suggested.

Sapphire bit her lip, thinking. "My absolute favorite thing to do is jump from the big rock by our house into the ocean. The best part is before you land in the water. It actually is like flying." Now she definitely felt better, remembering all that. But she still wasn't flying. She looked up at Comet to see her friend with a big, secretive smile on her face.

"You should for sure jump off something," Comet said. "I mean, you basically just described flying. That's what we need to do!"

"Makes sense to me!" Sapphire said. She and Comet tended to just go for things when they were alone together. She wondered what careful Twilight and Shamrock would say. But she shrugged it off. This was the day to take chances. She was discovering her magic!

"What about the bleachers?" Comet suggested.

Sapphire looked over. They didn't seem too high. Not high enough for her to get hurt, anyway. "Perfect," she said.

And that was how Sapphire found herself sprawled on the ground feeling very bruised.

"Sapphire! Are you okay?" Coach Ruby ran toward them from across the field. Even from far away they could feel her concern.

"I'm okay, Coach," Sapphire said, slowly getting back to her hooves, shaking off the fall.

"What in the five kingdoms were you doing?" Coach asked.

"Um, trying to see if I had a jumping strength?" Sapphire tried.

"Well, don't do that again." Coach Ruby laughed a little, relaxing after seeing that her player wasn't hurt. "Why don't you go see Stella and Celest? They can give you a tonic and make sure you're okay."

Stella and Celest did all the cooking for the school, and all the medical stuff, too.

"Oh, can I go too?" Comet asked. She spent a lot of time baking and cooking with them, even if she wasn't technically supposed to.

Coach Ruby shook her head. "Join up with Storm and Peppermint, and try to keep things safe this time."

"Maybe we can try to fly again later?" Comet asked Sapphire after Coach Ruby had left to help another teammate.

Sapphire shrugged. "No. I think we can agree that I do not have the gift of flight. But I wonder if Stella could help. I mean, she's a dragon! She has to know loads about traveling and magic."

Comet jumped up and hovered a little before landing back down with a thud. "Totally!"

Before she left, Sapphire took out her notebook and ink-well again and rested it on one of the benches. She crossed out "Learn to fly" and beneath it wrote, "Ask an expert."

6

Questing

On her way to the kitchens, Sapphire saw Shamrock in the Peony Pasture, examining something on the ground underneath the teachers' tree.

"Curiosity kills the quest." Sapphire sighed to herself, and headed toward Shamrock.

"What's up, Shamrock?" Sapphire stopped next to her friend and looked down where he was looking.

Shamrock jumped back in surprise and whipped his long silver mane around so that he could face Sapphire. Which in turn startled Sapphire, and she jumped back too.

After the giggles stopped, Shamrock put his serious face

back on. "Okay, but don't tell anyone," he said, looking around to make sure they were alone. "I wanted to see the fairy dust for myself, so I came investigating to see if any had leaked out, and sure enough there's a little pile right here. And it really does look just like powdered sugar!"

Sapphire could barely contain her excitement. A pile of magic right there?! She leaned over carefully and held her breath so as not to blow any away. She couldn't help but laugh when she realized what it was. "Shamrock! That looks like powdered sugar because it is!"

"No way. It isn't all sticky like when we used it for the class picture. That was more like paint."

"That's because it was mixed up with Twilight's sweat and, well, tears. This must have fallen off the candied apple Fairy Green was eating."

Shamrock raised his eyebrows. "I don't know . . . ," he began.

So Sapphire licked a little, not too much, in case it really was dust. But sure enough, it was sweet powdered sugar.

"Aw, man," Shamrock groaned. "I was so excited. I guess since I didn't get to go to the kitchens that time, I'm—um—not as familiar with the substance."

Sapphire laughed again. "Well, do you want to go now?" she asked. "Coach Ruby sent me to get a tonic and have a quick look-over to make sure I'm not hurt."

Shamrock looked up with concern, his bushy eyebrows popping out over his thick glasses. "What happened?"

"Oh, I'll explain on the way," Sapphire said.

★

Sapphire had just finished her tale when they reached the kitchen.

"Whoa, cool. I can't wait to see what Stella says. But, Sapphire, I don't think you need magic. I mean, you already can do everything. You're the smartest unicorn I know," Shamrock said.

"That's very nice," she said dismissively. "But I've started the quest for magic, Shamrock. And I need to finish it."

That was the type of logic Shamrock could understand, so he nodded supportively.

Looking up at the large, moss-covered building attached to a giant oak tree, Sapphire felt a rush of warmth. She loved the stitched bark walls and the chimney made of smooth, white pebbles. Of all the places at Unicorn U, this was where Sapphire felt most at home.

Sapphire used her glittering horn to knock three times on the huge oak door. Seconds later it swung open to reveal a smiling Stella and Celest.

"We heard you were coming!" boomed Stella, a small green dragon in a bright pink apron. "Coach Ruby sent a message ahead. But I see you stopped to grab a friend?"

Shamrock held his horn up high and gave her his "best student" look. "I'm Shamrock."

"Of course you are! We're happy to meet you," said Celest, a gray speckled unicorn with a curly, gray mane. "Come, come. It's too nice out for the kitchen," she said as she pushed Stella out the door. "Let's have our exam by the stream here. We even have some candied apples, so we can make a little picnic out of it." Stella held up an overflowing basket as proof.

Sapphire had never had so much fun at a doctor's appointment. Before long, the four of them were settled on a large blue-checkered picnic blanket. And Sapphire was deemed perfectly healthy.

"So, why were you really jumping off those bleachers, Sapphire?" Stella asked. As a dragon, Stella had a different type of magic and tended to see things that others missed. She could even see Twilight when she was fully invisible.

"Because . . . well, in order to become an explorer, I need to find my magic," Sapphire admitted. "Fairy Green said so today."

"I've met a few fairies in my day," Stella said. "But she is my absolute favorite." Stella stretched out and leaned against the tree, folding her scaly arms behind her so that her large head could rest on her hands. Her tail and legs were curled up beneath her.

"But what do you mean, find your magic?" Celest asked.

"My magical ability. Shamrock just discovered his yesterday, and now I'm on a quest to find mine."

Stella and Celest looked at each other, sharing their

special thing. It always seemed as if they could communicate with each other without speaking.

"Why don't we roast some marshmallows?" Celest suggested. "Stella, would you make the fire?"

"Oh! Could you teach me?" Sapphire asked. "That seems like a very important skill for an explorer."

Stella raised her scaly eyebrows in surprise. "No unicorn has ever asked me before! I'd love to." She took her claws from behind her head and sat up taller, clearly pleased by her own new adventure.

Shamrock and Sapphire smiled and inched closer to their dragon friend.

"To start, we'll need wood." Stella began her lesson. "Celest, could you grab some?"

"Of course," Celest agreed, disappearing into the house and quickly reappearing with a bundle of wood tied in an old red cloth. She had carried it with her horn and dumped it a few steps away from the picnic blanket.

Stella rumbled over to the wood, then settled herself on

her hind legs. Shamrock and Sapphire stood up and circled around.

"Every dragon can simply blow on a bundle of wood and make a fire," Stella told them. "But it is important that all of us learn to build a fire as well. It teaches us to respect the fire, which we dragons need for everything from food to building to communication. Fire is a very big deal for dragons."

Sapphire figured it was like water for her family. Everything about her life at home revolved around the ocean.

"Now, there are many ways for dragons to build fires. For example, I have fingers and scales and talons that can spark a flame. But there are hundreds of ways! I know them all."

Sapphire looked down at her hooves. She wasn't sure they would be very helpful.

"But there seems to be only one way a unicorn can build a fire without help," Celest joined in. "After all, we never used fire before the dragons showed us how. And we only really use it for cooking. In the north the long-haired unicorns use it for warmth only on the coldest days."

Shamrock and Sapphire nodded in unison. All the unicorns knew that their stoves were built by dragons, and designed so that the unicorns only needed to turn a little knob and—poof!—fire. And if they didn't have a stove, unicorns would use a special dragon-designed device that would turn sunlight into fire if held the right way.

"I'd love to go up north," Sapphire said. "I've never met a long-haired unicorn before. I wonder what their schools look like."

"I'm sure you'll see for yourself someday," Celest told her.

Stella took up the lesson. "For a unicorn to make a fire, you must have one rock the size of your hoof or bigger."

Celest demonstrated, knocking a big rock in front of her.

Sapphire smiled, watching the two of them. Celest and Stella seemed like one creature, half unicorn, half dragon. They wove their words and actions together like they were each one half of a whole.

"Then," Stella continued, "strike the rock with your horn in a curved motion so that a spark appears. We dragons do this with one of our claws."

Sapphire and Shamrock hurried to find their own rocks, eager to try to make a spark. Sapphire looked around for the perfect one. She figured it should have a flat side to rest on, so it didn't tip over went she struck it with her horn. After a bit of searching, she found exactly what she was looking for.

Celest demonstrated, and a spark appeared just as Stella had described. Sapphire and Shamrock tried to follow but only found themselves making terrible scraping noises against their own rocks.

Wincing at the noise, Celest offered some advice. "Try to make a *C* with your horn, and hit the rock at the very end of the curve."

This made perfect sense to Sapphire, and she did just that. She was pleased to see

a little spark appear in front of her. Shamrock didn't manage to create a spark, but he cheered along with Stella and Celest at Sapphire's success.

"Incredible, Sapphire!" Stella said, pleased with her new student. "I've never seen a unicorn pick that up so quickly. Now you'll need to gather some dried leaves from the ground, and some very small sticks. Add these to the pile of wood. I've already arranged the wood in the perfect pile, but that's a lesson for another day."

Sapphire gathered the required materials while Shamrock continued to work on his spark.

Once everything was put together, Stella continued the lesson. "Okay, now position your rock so the spark will meet with one of the dried materials and then the fire will catch."

Sapphire created a few sparks, and a small fire appeared in front of her. She was so happy, which made her think of Comet's doughnut story. She felt lighter than air.

The little group cheered again. "I am very impressed, Sapphire," Stella said. "You would fit right in with the dragons."

Sapphire grinned. She imagined herself surrounded by dragons, listening to them tell stories around a bonfire.

"Well done! It took me weeks to do it, really," Celest added.

"Thank you for teaching me, Stella and Celest," Sapphire said. "I have to admit, I feel kind of proud of myself."

Smiling, Sapphire took out her notebook and ink, and instead of crossing out "Ask an expert," she put a little check mark next to it. They may not have figured out her a magical ability, but she had learned something new.

7

Down to Earth

S he and Shamrock had science next and, after saying good-bye to Stella and Celest, headed to the Science Stables.

"I was thinking the Science Stables could inspire an earth element ability," Sapphire was saying.

"Well, you know, I think my photographic memory is related to the earth element. When I look at my memories, they all feel connected to living things, if that makes sense," Shamrock said.

"Actually, it does." Sapphire said, her investigator brain turning on. "How does the picture look when you see it? It is like a photograph? Or a painting?"

Shamrock thought about it. "It's like a photograph in the middle of the memory and a painting on the sides. Like, when I was looking for the basket of flowers, the flowers were a photograph but the surrounding details were more like a painting. I think it depends on what I'm focusing on. But the basket wasn't really clear. The flowers were much more clear. I think because they're rooted in the earth, you know?"

Sapphire nodded. "Totally." She and Shamrock were always able to understand each other. They just had the same logical brains. And before, they'd also been the only ones without a magical ability. Sapphire was happy for her friend, but she couldn't help feeling a little lonely and a little jealous. Those were new feelings for her, and she didn't like them. They felt sticky and uncomfortable. But it was like stepping into quicksand. She didn't know how to shake them off.

★

Professor Sherbet had just sent the science class to start working on their projects when she spotted Sapphire and

Shamrock walking toward the greenhouses. "Hi, you two!" she called.

"Stella and Celest sent word that you guys were on your way. Sounds like you had an extra lesson today." Professor Sherbet smiled at them.

The two students nodded. "Sapphire learned how to

make fire," Shamrock said. "I'm still figuring it out."

Sapphire wasn't paying attention. She was staring hard at the plants in front of her, biting her bottom lip the way she always did when hatching a plan.

"Sapphire? Hello?" Professor Sherbet waved her horn, gently shaking the moss crown on her head.

Sapphire was shaken out of her thoughts. "Sorry, Professor. I've been on a quest today. Would it be okay if Shamrock and I did a separate project right now? I have a burning question."

Professor Sherbet never could say no to a burning question. Like all the first years, Sapphire knew that the professor valued curiosity above all other things. The professor laughed, knowing too that all her students had learned how to pull at her heartstrings. "Oh, go ahead, you two. But I would like a full report of this quest at the end of the day, Sapphire."

★

Sapphire and Shamrock headed out of the greenhouse. She was feeling hopeful again.

"Don't you want to look at all the cools plants in there?" Shamrock asked.

Sapphire explained, "Remember Peppermint's story about waking up with her mother's knitting wrapped around her because she'd wanted a blanket?"

Shamrock nodded.

"And you developed your ability when Twilight, your friend, was in trouble."

"But I'm not sure where you're going with all this," he admitted.

"As unicorns, we are all connected to the earth. I mean, most of us have to walk on it, after all," Sapphire said. "So I think the earth element, for us anyway, has to do with what's familiar."

Shamrock nodded but his eyebrows were scrunched up, like he didn't quite get it.

"Well remember how I'm learning to weave new nets for Mom? She harvests seaweed and it feels like we're always having to repair the nets. I've been studying the books Mr. Jazz found on the strongest thread and weaving techniques and I started practicing the new weave with ivy and bark. I'm making them for my family so they're personal, and I was thinking maybe they could inspire some magic!"

Shamrock was now nodding in his usual enthusiastic way. "Sapphire, I think this is an important scientific discovery!"

With that, the two set off for the Silver Lining Stables at a friendly canter. Fast enough to get there quickly but slow enough to talk.

"What were you thinking about on the way to the Science Stables?" Sapphire asked. "Obviously you have something on your mind."

"I was actually thinking about that picture day," Shamrock said with a laugh. "I was using my ability to see it again. All that powdered sugar falling onto Twilight like snow. Comet a blur flying above her with that giant bag. It looked like a cloud. It was so fun to relive it all. And you were right, it wasn't sticky at all."

Sapphire cocked her head in confusion. Shamrock hadn't been at the bottom of the hill that day. She and Shamrock had helped Comet carry the bag of powdered sugar before she'd run up the hill with it to get her flying start. Twilight had described it in great detail, of course. But they hadn't actually seen the powdered sugar fall. Sapphire wanted to ask Shamrock questions, but before she had a chance, they saw Comet and Twilight racing toward them.

8

An Emergency

Comet and Twilight looked totally panicked as they rushed up them. Twilight's hooves were shimmering in and out of invisibility, and Comet was hovering over the ground.

"What's wrong?" Sapphire and Shamrock asked in unison. But no one laughed at the coincidence.

Instead Twilight squeaked, "Headmaster Starblaze has called for an emergency meeting on the Looping Lawn."

"Professor Sherbet told us you guys were doing a special project and to come get you right away," Comet explained.

"It's something to do with Fairy Green," Twilight added, her voice full of worry.

With that, the four unicorns cantered as fast as they could toward the Looping Lawn. Had something happened to their honored guest?

They arrived to see the whole campus gathered together in front of the large oak trees. Fairy Green's welcome banner still hung between them, making the whole thing seem sadder.

The teachers all flanked the headmaster, and Sapphire looked up to find Fairy Green perched atop Professor Sherbet's head, leaning back against her horn. She looked at home surround by the moss wreath, but her face was contorted with worry. Sapphire felt like something was missing, but what was it?

Headmaster Starblaze cleared his throat, and the whole university quieted down. "As most of you know," he began in his booming voice, "Unicorn U has had the great honor of hosting Fairy Green today." He paused and nodded toward the fairy, who bowed her small head in return.

"But a grave thing has happened during her time here," the headmaster continued. "Her basket of fairy dust has gone missing."

Sapphire felt tears well up. That basket was Fairy Green's most valuable possession. How would she get home without it? How would she travel? Sapphire wanted to help but didn't know how. *What can a first-year unicorn with no magic do?* Meanwhile, the school had erupted with chatter:

"Has someone taken it?"

"Where could it be?"

"I just saw her with it hours ago!"

"Who would've done such a thing?"

The headmaster stomped his front legs with such force that it felt as if the ground shook beneath them. The students immediately quieted.

"This fairy dust is not of use to unicorns, but it is of serious importance to fairies. Without this basket, Fairy Green will not be able to attend the annual Fairy Gathering, the most important day of the fairies' year. If anyone knows anything about this basket's whereabouts, please see one of your professors immediately. In the meantime, I have formed a search party of teachers. All students are to stay here on the lawn or in the Silver Lining Stables until the dinner bell. Classes have been canceled."

The professors gathered their classes together, doing their best to quiet the gossip and questions. With Fairy Green still perched on top of her head, Professor Sherbet led her students to a tree and asked her class to please wait quietly there while she and Fairy Green checked in with the headmaster. Somehow, Fairy Green seemed to have shrunk with sadness. The class did as they were told. They felt very protective of their fairy guest, and wanted to make her life easier.

But when the adults walked away, a discussion soon started up again.

"We need to do something!" Firefly shouted.

"Of course, but what can a bunch of first years do?" Peppermint asked.

"Well, remember what Flash said earlier today?" Storm asked. "We're the best first years she's seen. We have the best abilities, remember?"

Most of the class nodded in agreement, but some still argued that they should do as they were told.

Now Sapphire really felt she had nothing to offer Fairy Green or her classmates. It was clear the students with magical abilities were going to save the day, and she still hadn't found her magic. *I should get on with my quest*, she thought. Even if it was feeling less and less like she would ever find what she was looking for.

9

Hatching a Plan

S apphire! Come back!"

Sapphire turned to see her fellow students waving their horns her way. She sighed. *They probably just feel bad for me.*

Sapphire trotted back over to tell them not to worry about her, but her classmates didn't give her the chance.

"Um, where are you going?" Peppermint whined with a spectacular mane flip.

Sapphire took a deep breath and said, "Well, it's clear you don't need me, so—"

"Excuse me!" Comet said, floating slightly up from the ground. "You have been interrupting me all day, but I am going to say what I, and everyone else has been trying to say. We absolutely *do* need you. You're the glue!"

Sapphire rolled her eyes. She was sick of everyone trying to make her feel better. It actually made her angry. She just couldn't take it anymore.

Hot tears welled up as she yelled, "Ugh! You guys obviously do not need me. I have NO magic. I can't fly around campus and look for the basket from the air, like you, Comet. I can't listen in on conversations to see if anyone really did take the basket, like you can, Twilight. I can't call the wind to sweep back the long grass and see if it's hidden in there, like you can, Storm. And I definitely can't take down everyone's memories from the day and use my ability to see when the basket went missing, like you can, Shamrock!" Sapphire finished her rant. She was panting now. All her angry energy had been expelled, like she'd let out all the air from a balloon and was just deflated. She needed a nap. But when she looked up at her classmates, she saw them all smiling at her. "What?" she snapped. Had they not heard her?

It was Twilight who was brave enough to come closer

to the fuming Sapphire. "Well, it seems like you might have a plan for how to save the day. Want to walk us through it? Um, perhaps a bit more calmly and slowly this time?" Twilight smiled and, so only Sapphire could see, winked.

It took Sapphire a minute to work out what Twilight meant. "Well, let's start with Shamrock," she said, a little hesitantly.

"Yeah, what in the kingdoms were you talking about?" he asked.

"Well, I think you might be able to patch together memories that aren't yours into your . . . What did you call it? Memory movie?"

Shamrock nodded.

"Okay, well, I was thinking of when you told me about reliving the time when Comet poured powdered sugar all over Twilight. You actually didn't see that, remember? We were on the other side of the hill. But Twilight told us about it. I think you were able to access her memory when she shared it somehow, and add it to the movie."

It was like the class was watching a hoofball match. As soon as Sapphire stopped talking, they all turned to Shamrock at once, wondering if it was true.

Shamrock's glasses shook up and down his nose as he nodded, taking in what she was saying. "Oh my glitter, you're right! And if enough unicorns tell me exactly when and where they saw Fairy Green, I should be able to put together a mental movie of the day!"

It seemed both sides had won this match, as the whole

class cheered together. Everyone gathered in a line, eager to share their stories with Shamrock.

When the class had finished, Shamrock closed his eyes. Breathing in and out, he took his time putting the memories together. Finally he opened his eyes to look at everyone. But he had a heavy frown, and his eyebrows were pushed low enough to be entirely hidden by his glasses. It didn't seem as if he had succeeded.

Sapphire, who was starting to feel like her old self again, walked over with confidence. "Think about the earth," she suggested. "Think about the trees and flowers and grass included in their memories. Think painting, not movie."

Shamrock smiled at her, and closed his eyes again. The class waited silently for what felt like hours but was only a few minutes. Then Shamrock opened his eyes. This time triumph was shining through.

"Okay," Shamrock said. "It seems that no one has seen the basket since Fairy Green flew over the Spotlight Flowers. That was when she was also carrying a bunch of baskets from Stella and Celest, so it would make sense if she didn't notice one of them drop."

Sapphire smiled, picking up where he was going. "And since Spotlight Flowers close whenever someone is near, they may have closed up right over the basket."

The class cheered again. They'd figured it out!

"Um, excuse me!" Peppermint called out. "Does no one else see the problem? The Spotlight Garden is humungous. How is Twilight supposed to search the area all by herself? And I'm pretty sure she's the only invisible unicorn in the whole school."

"Actually, I have a plan for that," Sapphire said. She grinned, and her friends noticed that the sparkle in her eye was back. And it might just have been bigger than ever.

10

A Search Party

Sapphire, Comet, Twilight, and Shamrock got ready for their new quest. Students were supposed to be staying on the Looping Lawn, so this was going to have to be a covert mission. A herd of first years was not going to go unnoticed.

Before the group left, Peppermint wove a long length of ivy around Comet's waist. She even wove some flowers through it, making it almost as beautiful as her welcome banner. "What?" Peppermint asked when she saw Sapphire's face. "Just because it's practical doesn't mean it has to be boring."

Sapphire just shrugged.

When everyone was ready, Sapphire gave Storm the signal—two stomps and a whinny.

Storm called up a wicked wind and whipped it into a small tornado. The spiral wiggled through the lawn, drawing everyone's attention. Just like it was supposed to.

Sapphire and her rescue team made their escape. Keeping off the main paths, and sticking to the woods, they made their way to the Spotlight Garden.

★

"Okay, Fairy Green was seen flying into the Spotlight Garden from this side, so I think we should start here. She was next seen at the Science Stables, so head in that direction, Twilight," Shamrock told her.

Sapphire handed Twilight one end of the ivy. The other was still tied around Comet's waist. "Hold this in your mouth, Twilight, and be careful not to let it touch the ground."

"Okay," Twilight said, looking nervous about the important part she had to play.

"You can totally do this," Sapphire assured her.

Twilight smiled at Sapphire before she closed her eyes, and soon enough she disappeared from view. Even though they'd seen it a million times by now, her friends were always astounded at how good she was at disappearing. She was really starting to master this ability. *A long way from the first day*, Sapphire thought.

"Here I go," invisible Twilight told them, her voice muffled by the ivy rope.

"Then I guess that's my cue," Comet said. She was

already floating in excitement, so she just pedaled her legs as if she were swimming in air, and rose higher. Soon she was well above the other unicorns' heads.

"Comet! Stop pedaling. Let Twilight pull you. Just focus on finding the basket!" Sapphire reminded her.

"Right-o, Captain!" Comet yelled from above, and she did start searching below.

Sapphire and Shamrock waited nervously, both wiggling in anticipation, until finally Comet called, "Twilight! Twilight! Turn around and walk three steps back. There's the basket!"

And just moments later, Fairy Green's bark basket was floating over the Spotlight Flowers as Comet flew above.

"You know, it's really quite something to see the world from up here," Comet called down to them all.

11

The Fairy Good Return

The students on the Looping Lawn greeted the four friends with big cheers. Some older students even started the chant "Best first years ever!"

But the teachers did not seem to be in the same mood. Even Professor Sherbet looked disappointed. "You should not have done that on your own," she told them in a very serious voice. "You should always tell a teacher."

"Your teacher is right. It is important to listen to your elders," Fairy Green added, still sitting on Professor Sherbet's head.

All at once Sapphire, Shamrock, Twilight, and Comet started talking.

"It was all in the name of the school," Shamrock tried to argue.

"Please don't be angry! Please, please, please!" Comet pleaded.

Twilight mumbled something no one could understand.

It was Sapphire who stepped forward calmly. "It was my idea, Professor," she said with her head held high. Her heart was beating wildly and she wanted to bite her lip. But she willed herself to stand up for their plan, and protect her friends. She looked first into the eyes of Professor Sherbet. "It was my plan, Professor, the whole thing." Then, though it felt as if her body were frozen in fear, she turned toward the headmaster. "None of the other students should be punished. I convinced them to do it." And finally, even though it now felt as if Storm had sent icy rain to keep her from looking up, Sapphire made herself look into Fairy Green's eyes to say, "I think your class today may have changed my whole life. And I didn't want you to think badly about our school. And I didn't want you to miss the gathering. So I don't regret what we did. I'm happy you have your basket again."

Fairy Green and Professor Sherbet smiled at Sapphire with such warmth that they made her feel like they'd asked the sun to melt all that ice away and fill her up with sunshine.

But the headmaster did not seem at all moved by her words. "Please come to my office, Sapphire." He turned without even looking to make sure she followed him.

"After you speak with your headmaster," Fairy Green told her, "I do hope we can have a chance to talk before I leave."

Sapphire could only stare in wonder at such an opportunity. If she had to get through a lecture to talk to Fairy Green, she would. That gave her all the bravery she needed. With a deep breath, Sapphire squared her shoulders and followed the headmaster.

The headmaster's office was not the scary place she'd expected. She didn't know what exactly she *had* expected, but it wasn't this cozy room. There wasn't even a desk! Just a large rug and a fireplace. The walls were lined with book hooks and paintings of all different sizes and in all different styles of art. The books too seemed to be a mix of things.

There were fantasy stories and textbooks, dictionaries and thrillers. *Who is this unicorn?* Sapphire wondered.

"Are you ready now?"

Sapphire jumped back a little. She hadn't realized how long she'd been staring at his things. "Oh, um, yes, Headmaster, sir," she said as confidently as she could manage.

Headmaster Starblaze surprised her even further by chuckling softly. "Now, now, you're not in trouble, Sapphire. In fact, I would like to thank you."

"But, Headmaster. Before—it seemed, well, like you were going to expel me."

"You did break the rules. You and your fellow first years will have to receive some sort of punishment. I'll think on that. But for now I'd like to offer my thanks. Your search party proved much more successful than mine. And I do believe you have helped the five kingdoms because of it."

"Well, thank you, sir," Sapphire said, feeling about a million times better. She wanted to tell him it was all because of her classmates' abilities, but she didn't want to get them

in any more trouble. Plus, she was beginning to realize that she'd played a big part in finding the basket. Perhaps the biggest of all.

"Okay, that is all. You may rejoin your friends, Sapphire."

Sapphire turned to go, but, curiosity getting the best of her, she turned back around and asked, "Headmaster, what's your ability?"

The headmaster looked taken aback. "No one has ever asked me before," he said.

Sapphire laughed. He was the third person to say that to her that day.

"Well, since no one knows, all the students think it must be something very impressive. Or terrible."

The headmaster threw back his head and laughed so hard, the picture frames shook on the walls. When he finally stopped, he said, "I don't have an ability, Sapphire. It's just me."

"You know what? I don't think I have one either," Sapphire admitted, and she turned around and left the office. She skipped all the way out, feeling lighter than air.

★

Before she got back to the Looping Lawn, Sapphire saw Fairy Green flying her way. The fairy had her basket securely over her shoulder and was carrying a tiny suitcase. "Sapphire!" she called out.

Sapphire went over to her. The dancing beans from earlier felt like they had found their way back to her hooves. She skidded to a stop in front of the fairy, catching herself from falling just in time.

"I wanted to clarify my answer from this morning, Sapphire," Fairy Green said.

Sapphire hadn't been expecting that. She could only blink in surprise.

"I want you to know that you have magic, Sapphire. And certainly enough to travel the five kingdoms. Magic comes in so many forms. Sometimes as dust. Sometimes as flashy unicorn abilities. And sometimes it comes in the form of leadership, curiosity, or a good heart. And you have all three of those."

Sapphire was speechless. It was the kindest thing anyone

had ever said. "Uh—thank you, Fairy Green," she finally managed.

"Oh, and that's the other thing. My real name is 'Juniper.' Now that you know it, you can call on me and I'll hear it wherever I am. If you ever need me, just say my name and I'll find you."

"Thank you very much, Juniper. I am honored," Sapphire said, tears of pride brimming in her eyes.

And with that, Juniper sprinkled some fairy dust and disappeared with a pop.

Sapphire looked up to see her friends waving from up on the hill. Looking at them, she realized that it wasn't their abilities that made them special. Not at all. They were magical because of the unicorns they were. Sapphire took out her notebook and wrote "Magic found" and underlined it.

Smiling, she galloped over to her friends and wondered what kind of adventure they were going to go on next.

Shamrock's
Seaside Sleepover

1

Up and Away!

Shamrock peered through his thick, black-rimmed glasses at his space-themed backpack. Sprinkled all over the pack were tiny glow-in-the-dark stars, which matched the rest of his room. Bright orange, red, and purple planets hung from the ceiling on strings, and a telescope was arranged by his window, pointing toward the sky. Shamrock was always reading about the discoveries of famous unicorn astronomers, and dreamt of making his own discoveries one day. He *loved* facts and wanted to know how the whole universe worked.

Tapping his front hoof, Shamrock tried to think of what else he'd need for Sapphire's sleepover party. Should he bring the telescope with him? He'd never been to a sleepover before, but he had read about them in books and was pretty sure he knew how it would go. Sapphire lived at the beach, so they would probably explore the seaside caves during the day and study the stars at night. Comet and Twilight, Shamrock's other best friends, would also be there. Knowing Comet, she would bring delicious treats that she had baked herself. Still, Shamrock couldn't help but feel a little nervous. He knew the other three unicorns had been to sleepovers before. He hoped he wouldn't be terribly out of the loop.

Shamrock decided they would take turns with Sapphire's telescope, so there was no need to bring his own. But he did pack his brand-new, very favorite book. Using his horn, he grabbed *1,000 Incredible and Astonishing Facts* from his book hook. When in doubt, he knew he could dazzle his friends with new facts.

"Shamrock! Time to go!" Dad called out.

"We don't want to fly this thing in the dark, remember!" he heard his Pop add.

Shamrock and his dads lived high up on a mountain and used a hot-air balloon for travel. Otherwise it would take weeks to get anywhere!

"Coming!" Shamrock yelled back. At this point, he could only hope he was prepared.

He zipped the pack up with his mouth, slipped his head through the long loop, and hurried toward the front door. Through the door's window, he could see that his parents were already waiting on the lawn. Even though he was used to it, Shamrock was still impressed by the bright rainbow colors of the balloon. It billowed and waved in the wind, looking eager to rise up into the sky. The huge basket was held in place by large ropes attached to spikes in the ground.

Shamrock trotted out to join his family. His dads walked into the basket and started undoing the ropes. Shamrock followed, closed the door behind him, and made himself cozy. Pop, who was always thinking ahead like Shamrock, had loaded the basket with blankets and pillows to make the journey comfortable.

Dad untied the big ropes, and they were off. Floating

high above Sunshine Springs, Shamrock watched the mountains get smaller and smaller as they made their way over little towns and winding roads. To the north, he could spot the hill that Unicorn University, his school, stood atop. But they were headed south to the ocean. They passed fields that looked like his patched-up quilt back home, and they passed by cotton-candy clouds. Shamrock felt his heart soar. He looked up to see Dad adjusting the flame above their heads. Shamrock knew that the flame heated up the air inside the balloon (which he also knew was technically called the envelope) and that hot air was lighter than cold air, which was why hot-air balloons could float! Shamrock smiled at himself. The science of the hot-air balloon was really magical. He loved flying.

Soon enough he could see the sparkling, deep blue ocean waves whooshing and washing over the beach that Sapphire lived by. It was time for Shamrock's first sleepover. A seaside sleepover!

2

Good-Byes and Hellos

The white sand was nearly below them as Shamrock's dad turned down the flame enough to lower the basket over the beach. The sun was low in the sky, painting the clouds different colors, like a big bowl of rainbow sherbet.

"Okay, Shamrock, we're going to dip low on the sand, and you jump out," his dad was telling him. "We'll be back on Sunday to pick you up."

"Have so much fun, Son!" Pop said with a smile. He gave Shamrock a good-bye nuzzle. "We can't wait to hear all about it. And look, there are Comet, Sapphire, and Twilight now!"

Shamrock's heart leapt when he saw his friends running

down the beach to meet him. Finally the basket got low enough for Shamrock to jump out to a chorus of good-byes from his dads and hellos from his friends.

Shamrock tried to tell his friends an awesome sunset fact he'd read about in *1,000 Incredible and Astonishing Facts* when he landed on the beach, but everyone started talking at once. Comet was shouting about a new pumpkin cupcake recipe she'd recently tried, Twilight was trying to tell them about her new art project, and Sapphire was attempting to herd them to the tent. It was a happy, confusing reunion.

Even though fall break had just started a few days before, Shamrock felt like he hadn't seen his best friends in ages. He was so excited to be with them, it felt like he was still floating in the hot-air balloon. His face almost hurt because he was smiling so big.

"You guys won't believe the tent Sapphire put together," Twilight said when everyone quieted down. Twilight had a jet-black coat, and today her hooves were a sunshine yellow. She painted them different colors all the time, and Shamrock always admired them. She lived much closer to

Sapphire than the others did and must have walked over with her parents earlier in the day.

"Let's go now!" Comet, a rose-colored unicorn, cheered. She was floating with anticipation. Really! Comet had the power of flight. When Shamrock asked how she had traveled, Comet told him that she and her uncle had flown over and arrived just before Shamrock.

"Follow me," Sapphire said with a proud grin. The four of them trotted down the beach to a grassy bank where a large, red barn stood.

"That's where we live!" Sapphire said, pointing to the barn with her horn. "But this is where we'll stay!" She trotted over to a big blue tent. Her blue coat matched it so well, she almost blended in.

Wow. Shamrock was impressed by what his friend had done. String lights were hung up around the tent, and brightly colored rugs and pillows were arranged to make a sort of outdoor living room. In front, she'd made a firepit and even put out sticks and buckets of marshmallows. Shamrock only wondered where the telescope was.

"This is so cool," Comet said. "I've never been camp-
ing before!"

"I'm glad you like it. I've been working on it all day,"
Sapphire said. "But the best part is that my uncle Sea Star
is in town. He's taking my sisters out on his ship right now,
but they should be back any minute. He tells the best stories.
You're all going to love him!"

Just as Sapphire finished speaking, a large, gray unicorn
came rambling over. He wore his mane in loose braids like

Sapphire's and had one large, gold earring and a red bandanna tied around his neck. He chuckled. "Are you talking about me?"

"Uncle Sea Star! You're back!" Sapphire said.

Shamrock noticed that four miniature versions of Sapphire had followed Uncle Sea Star over to the tent. They were all talking at once about their boat ride, and it was hard to hear what anyone was saying. Shamrock smiled. This was way different from how it was at his home. He and his dads were usually pretty quiet. Sapphire introduced Uncle Sea Star and her siblings—Ruby, Amber, Opal, and Gem—to her friends.

"Okay, everyone! Come inside for dinner," a voice called from the red barn.

Shamrock looked up to see a light blue unicorn with a white mane standing in the open barn door, an apron hanging from her neck.

"Coming, Mom!" Sapphire shouted before turning back to her friends. "Come on! You're going to love my mom's famous seaweed soup." Sapphire was saying that they were going to love a lot of things, and Shamrock believed her. His first sleepover was off to a great start.

The barn's kitchen was huge, with big windows in the ceiling that you could see the first few stars of the night shine through. Everyone was gathered around a long, wooden table that looked like it was made of driftwood. They were so close to the ocean that you could even hear the waves. Well, only when everyone was slurping their soup and not talking. The soup was salty and delicious and unlike anything Shamrock had ever had before.

Comet licked up the last drop from her bowl and leaned back happily. "I have to have this recipe!"

"I know," Shamrock agreed. "Is this a special seaweed?"

"It's from the bay right there. I gathered it this morning," Sapphire's mom told them. "Seaweed is always better when it's fresh."

"You know, I once knew a unicorn who traveled the world and never went anywhere without a jar of salt water from the bay where she grew up," Uncle Sea Star said, pushing his own bowl away from him. "Said it kept her mind fresh."

From there, Uncle Sea Star's story about the unicorn with the saltwater jar took many twists and turns that Shamrock did not find very believable, but he tried to be polite and listen without interrupting. Shamrock couldn't help himself, though, when Uncle Sea Star said the unicorn had lived to be a thousand years old because of the water.

"That's impossible!" Shamrock burst out, surprising everyone at the table.

"Perhaps," Uncle Sea Star said with a grin. "Though, sea legends can have more truth to them than you might think."

Shamrock didn't know what to think, so he looked over at Sapphire, who just shrugged and smiled admiringly at Uncle Sea Star.

After dinner, Sapphire's younger sisters went up to hear a bedtime story from their mom, and Shamrock and his friends went outside to roast marshmallows. Uncle Sea Star built a roaring fire and asked them if they'd like to hear a ghost story.

Comet and Sapphire gave an enthusiastic "YES!" Shamrock thought Uncle Sea Star's stories seemed too fantastical, like they were tales for Sapphire's younger sisters, not older kids who knew things about the world. But when everyone settled on the grass, Shamrock kept quiet and sat down next to Twilight.

The young unicorns waited as Uncle Sea Star gazed into the fire, clearly deep in thought. *Probably making up a story on the spot,* Shamrock said to himself. It was a cloudy night, and the stars peeked through the dark gray wisps in the sky. The waves washed ashore, creating gentle background music, and the peeping bugs got quieter, as if they were getting ready for the story too. The fire glowed brightly in the center of their small circle and crackled here and there. Shamrock had to admit, it *was* the perfect setting for a story. *If only it were true,* he thought.

Uncle Sea Star leaned back against a large boulder. "All

righty. This is the oldest sea legend I know," he began. "I think I first heard it when I was your age."

Here we go, Shamrock thought. *Uncle Sea Star must think we're a bunch of little ponies.*

"Legend has it that for as long as there've been unicorns living by the ocean," Uncle Sea Star said, "the Glowing Horn has been floating along our shores, protecting an unknown treasure. Many, many unicorns have seen it when they've been out at sea. Even I have seen the Glowing Horn on a misty night—"

"Oh, come on!" Shamrock grumbled, unable to keep quiet any longer. "You did not *really* see a ghost."

"Shush, Shamrock," Comet said. "He's telling the story!"

Shamrock felt his cheeks flush. That wasn't very nice of him to interrupt Uncle Sea Star. "Sorry," he said softly.

"It's true, I really did see it," Uncle Sea Star continued. "It was at night, when the moon was but a sliver and the water was as black as ink. At first I didn't believe it either. I thought it was just my eyes getting tired, but I blinked and I rubbed and—sure as seashells—there was a bright Glowing Horn bobbing in the waves. I knew then, as I know now, that the old story says that whoever reaches the Glowing Horn will find unknown treasure."

Uncle Sea Star paused for a moment and looked out to the ocean. The silence stretched on for what felt like forever. Sapphire whinnied impatiently.

"Tell us more about the treasure," Comet blurted out. Even Twilight looked interested.

Shamrock wasn't sure why, but it made him mad that Uncle Sea Star was pretending to tell the truth when this was all make-believe. He couldn't help but push back. "Well, where's the treasure now?" he asked.

Shamrock was pretty sure that was rude too and felt a little bad about it. Uncle Sea Star was being nice, after all. But Shamrock couldn't stand hearing a story so clearly not based in fact. Uncle Sea Star just looked at him and smiled. "I never went after the horn."

"What? Why not?" Comet almost sounded mad.

"Because every unicorn that has been lured into the sea

by the Glowing Horn's treasure has never been seen again!"

All four unicorn friends jumped back. Even Shamrock! Then they giggled at themselves. Uncle Sea Star chuckled along with them. "All right, time for bed, kids. I'll be out in the morning getting some new supplies for my next sea voyage, but I'll see you for dinner tomorrow." With that, he walked back to the big barn. Even if the whole thing was made up, Shamrock had to admit that Uncle Sea Star could tell a good story.

Shamrock was too tired to even suggest looking through a telescope, and he could tell his friends were sleepy too. So he followed Sapphire to the tent, where everyone settled into their blankets and pillows. The others kept whispering about treasure and ghosts. Shamrock was a little annoyed by how they all seemed to believe Uncle Sea Star's story, when he knew they were smarter than that. Soon enough, their conversation ended, and he could hear Comet's soft snores. Shamrock snuggled in with *1,000 Incredible and Astonishing Facts* to read some true stories before falling asleep.

3

Beach Day Blues

The next morning, Shamrock woke up to the sounds of his friends laughing. He sat up, seeing that everyone was still in tangles of blankets and pillows. The morning air was crisp and cool, so Shamrock snuggled back into his own cozy blanket.

"I dreamt about ghosts all night," Twilight was saying, her eyes big. "I kept thinking there was a Glowing Horn in the tent!" She shuddered.

"Out of everyone, I thought you would be the least afraid of ghosts, Twilight," Sapphire said.

"What do you mean?" Shamrock asked, sitting up. He

yawned and put on his glasses. *Maybe Sapphire will be reasonable about this ghost business.*

"Well, Twilight's ability is sort of ghosty. When she's invisible, we can't see her, but we can hear her!" Sapphire explained.

"It is not the same!" Twilight screeched.

Comet laughed. "Of course it's not! 'Cause you're aliiiiivve!" Comet said the last part like she was telling a scary story of her own, and all the friends started laughing.

One of Sapphire's sisters came in to tell them that breakfast was ready. They followed her into the barn for a breakfast of kelp muffins topped with melting butter. Shamrock ate four.

"I'm going to look for the Glowing Horn today," Comet announced as the four friends walked down to the beach.

"Don't do it!" Twilight warned as they wove their way through the tall grass. "I mean, you don't want to be lured out to sea forever, do you?"

"She's right," Sapphire agreed, and looked back at them. She was leading everyone to a special secret beach she'd told them about at breakfast. "All the treasure stories around here

always lead to bad things. Trust me, I've heard a lot of them."

Shamrock took a deep breath. "Guys, there is no evidence that ghosts are real. In fact, these stories usually hide real scientific truths. So they're kind of dangerous. I've been meaning to show you this new book I have, *1,000 Incredible and Astonishing Facts*—"

But Comet didn't let him finish. "Actually, I have a theory about the ghost."

Not only did she interrupt him but she ignored him too. Shamrock felt like she had taken all the wind out of his hot-air balloon, but Comet didn't seem to notice. *Maybe I just didn't say it loudly enough,* he thought.

"The story says you can't go *after* the ghost," she continued, "but what about *inviting* the ghost to shore?"

"Guys!" Shamrock yelled this time. "Ghosts are not real. We know this. However, I've done research on the caves here, and there are stones in there that are way more interesting than any ghost. Some of them even sparkle in the dark, without sunlight! Why don't we go rock hunting instead of ghost hunting?"

Shamrock looked around at his friends, expecting to see their faces lighting up with excitement. But they didn't seem to get it. He felt his heart sink with disappointment.

Sapphire said, "Let's hang on the beach for a little while. I brought a blanket and a hoofball." Sapphire held up her basket so he could see. "There are some cool shells around here, though!"

Shamrock was bummed, but Comet and Twilight were already helping Sapphire set up the beach blanket, and at least this did not involve silly ghost hunting.

"Ooh, and your mom packed us some more of the kelp muffins," Comet said, bringing out her own basket. "I'm pretty sure I'll eat ten today."

They lounged and laughed on the beach, and Shamrock had to admit that it was fun, even if there weren't any special rocks around. He got out his copy of *1,000 Incredible and Astonishing Facts* and showed it to Sapphire.

"This is so cool, Shamrock!" Sapphire was as excited as he was about it. "Actually, I kind of wonder what it says about ghosts."

Shamrock groaned.

"I can tell you about a ghost," Comet told them. "Once, when I was staying at my great-aunt Jupiter's, I was sleeping on the couch, and I swear I saw an old bathrobe dancing on its own in the middle of the night. Just swirling around the living room!"

Twilight laughed so much, she spit out some of her muffin, and Sapphire snorted. But Shamrock was totally over the ghost talk.

"Comet, you know you were only dreaming," he said. "There's never been any evidence of ghosts. It's just stories people like to tell."

"I don't know, Shamrock," Twilight said. "I think I believe in ghosts. I mean, if there are so many stories about them, that's kind of like evidence, right?"

Comet nodded enthusiastically. "Totally, Twilight! Good point."

Sapphire shook her head. "Honestly, I'm with Shamrock. I mean, I've heard sea legends like this all my life, and I love them. But I just think people like to tell stories, and ghosts always make for good ones."

Shamrock nodded, feeling much better. At least someone was on his side. He stood up and kicked the hoofball. "Who wants to play?" he asked.

"Me!" Comet said, and Shamrock passed it to her. Twilight and Sapphire ran down the beach and drew a goal in the sand. Comet and Shamrock did the same where they were.

Comet and Sapphire were on Unicorn University's hoofball team and were better players than Twilight and Shamrock, but it was still fun running on the beach and scoring goals in the sand.

After a while, Comet stopped dribbling the ball to say, "Can we break for some more of those seaweed muffins? All this running has made me hungry."

Shamrock heard his belly rumble. "I wouldn't mind a muffin break," he said.

Twilight took the ball from Comet and tried to kick it in the direction of the picnic blanket, but—oh no!—it went zooming toward Sapphire's head.

"Sapphire, look out!" Twilight squeaked, but Sapphire didn't seem to hear her. She didn't even notice when the ball zoomed right by her ear.

Shamrock saw that Sapphire was staring out at the

ocean. Her face was so pale that it looked like—well, like she'd seen a ghost!

Sapphire shook her head and looked over to her friends. "You guys, you won't believe this, but I think I just saw the Glowing Horn."

4

Follow That Horn!

Sapphire dashed along the beach, toward the direction of the barn. "I think it went this way!" she shouted behind her. "Let's follow it!"

Twilight and Comet galloped after her, with Shamrock following behind. He hoped his book wouldn't get soaked by a wave while he was gone. Sapphire was clearly just imagining things because they had talked about ghosts all morning! No way was there an actual Glowing Horn—today, or ever.

They raced back and forth along the water, everyone peering out to see if they could find the horn again, but no one saw anything.

Finally Sapphire gave up the search and stopped running.

But she still had a huge smile on her face and a glimmer in her eye. Shamrock, like Comet and Twilight, knew that was her adventure face.

"Operation Sleepover Ghost Hunt, am I right?" Comet said with excitement. It wasn't quite a shout, but Comet had a naturally loud voice that always sounded a little like she was yelling at a hoofball game.

Twilight laughed. "This better not be a scary ghost."

"You guys are being way too silly," Shamrock said. This was totally out of control. "Ghosts are not real. I have tons of books that say so."

"You aren't being very open-minded, Shamrock," Sapphire pointed out.

"You were just saying you didn't believe in ghosts!" Shamrock insisted.

"Seems like a lifetime ago," Sapphire said simply. "Not to mention, I just had firsthand experience with one. You know that observation is a basic principle of scientific discovery."

That stopped Shamrock in his tracks. He bit his bottom

lip and nodded his mint-colored head. Perhaps he had been thinking about this ghost business all wrong. Maybe the best way to put this ghost behind them and move on to the caves was to *prove* to his friends that the ghost was all in their imaginations. He gave his friends a serious look that they all knew as "Shamrock Science Mode."

"Okay, let's scientific-method this ghost," he said with a smile.

Everyone laughed and cheered.

"But after we figure out what's going on with the ghost, do you guys promise to explore the caves with me?" he asked.

They all agreed and did a group high-U to seal the deal.

Shamrock said, "Okay, well, we have our scientific question: 'Are ghosts real?'" Everyone else groaned, but he ignored them. "The next step is to gather information."

"Glitter-tastic! We should talk to Uncle Sea Star," Comet said. "Maybe there's some information he left out. Maybe he even knows how to talk to ghosts."

"Let's go meet him in town," Sapphire agreed. "You

guys will love it. It's the oldest town in Sunshine Springs!"

They walked away from the water and through the tall beach grasses. Shamrock was excited. He wondered what kind of old buildings there would be and if there was anything about them in *1,000 Incredible and Astonishing Facts.*

"I'm thinking we should have a nice, polite chat with the horn," Comet said as they walked along the winding lane filled with broken seashells.

"How would a floating horn be able to talk?" Shamrock asked.

Comet shrugged, but Twilight said, "There are more ways to communicate than just speaking. Maybe the horn can spell out words or move objects."

"Very true," said Comet. "So we'll figure out how to talk to the horn, and then we will ask it to join us on the beach. *Then* we will ask it where the treasure is."

"And we won't get lost at sea, because we're luring the ghost to *us*!" Sapphire said. "Brilliant, Comet."

"I don't know," Twilight said softly. "What if we make friends with the ghost and leave the treasure alone?"

"Let's take the scientific method step-by-step. We don't have to worry about the treasure yet," Shamrock pointed out.

The sun was shining, and the ocean breeze was cool. The four friends were enjoying the walk so much that they made it to town before long and were all smiling as they wove their way through the cluster of little wooden buildings.

Shamrock noticed that the whole town seemed to lean east, as if the ocean wind had pushed it that way. Most houses had sea glass windows, with different blues and greens melted together. Unicorns were selling rope, seaweed, and trinkets from carts that lined the roads. Shamrock saw one unicorn push a cart filled with old books. The pages were browned with age, and it looked like the covers were made of everything from old sails to dried bark.

"Hey, kids! Looking for me?" The friends spun around, and Uncle Sea Star was standing right in front them, a big basket full of rope hanging from his neck.

"Uncle Sea Star, I have incredible news," Sapphire told him in her serious student voice.

Then Comet yelled out, "She saw the Glowing Horn!

She saw the Glowing Horn!" until Sapphire shushed her in an equally loud voice.

Shamrock looked around to see the unicorns of the town peeking at his friends curiously. There was a very old unicorn pushing a cart of glass bottles and iron pots and pans who looked particularly interested. Two unicorns dressed like Uncle Sea Star stopped their conversation and pricked up their ears. Shamrock was curious about what Uncle Sea Star knew too.

"Uncle Sea Star, you have to tell us how to lure the horn to the beach," Sapphire was saying. "Think of the treasure!"

Uncle Sea Star chuckled. "This is a treasure-hunting sleepover, eh? No, no. Too many unicorns have been lost to this legend. You'll just have to let the horn be, niece."

"But I found a loophole!" Comet pressed. "If we lure the horn to us, then the horn can't lure us to the sea." She closed her eyes and nodded seriously, as if settling the point.

Uncle Sea Star just shook his head. Shamrock knew his friends were going about this all wrong. If he were going to be part of this fact-finding mission, then they were going to do things correctly.

"Right now we're just gathering information to form our hypothesis," Shamrock said seriously. "That means 'an educated guess,' by the way. We will not perform any experiments until we get our facts straight, I promise. Of course, we'd rather talk to you about this instead of finding the information someplace else. I mean, some of those

old books over on that cart looked like they might have some information . . . and actually, those unicorns over there seemed interested. . . ." Shamrock drifted off, starting to get lost in thought. He wished they were closer to the library at school.

Uncle Sea Star chuckled and shook his head again. "Okay, okay, but this is just an old story, all right? Might not be anything to it. And all four of you must promise me you won't get yourselves into any danger. Sapphire, don't get me in trouble with your mother!"

Sapphire promised not to do anything dangerous.

Uncle Sea Star nodded and said, "Legend says that the Glowing Horn is always trying to add to its treasure. It's supposed to be drawn to shiny things."

The young unicorns nodded in unison, hanging on his every word.

"The thing is, the Glowing Horn knows unicorns want to take its treasure. Make sure it doesn't see you, or else you could be in trouble with the ghost!"

Twilight sighed.

Sapphire ignored it. "Twilight, I think we'll need to use your special powers."

"I was afraid you were going to say that," Twilight said, shaking her head.

Before any of them could thank Uncle Sea Star for his very valuable information or even say good-bye, he was crossing the street, waving his horn to a unicorn with an eye patch and a very dirty apron.

5

Finding Treasure

Okay, so what do we do to find this treasure?" Comet asked as they walked away from town.

Shamrock said, "Well, we can all agree that we have different theories for how this will turn out—"

"We'll be rich, with treasure!" Comet shouted.

"We'll discover something valuable, at the very least," Sapphire said with confidence.

"We'll make a new ghost friend," Twilight said softly.

Shamrock just nodded. They all knew what his theory was. "The next logical step is to conduct an experiment. Normally this would take weeks of planning, but I'm willing to cut some corners to keep the process moving. Does anyone have any ideas?"

Twilight mumbled, "I think Sapphire does."

"I do!" Sapphire said, nudging Twilight gently with her flank. "We go down to the beach tonight. Twilight will use her invisibility to set out a bunch of sparkly things in front of a fire, so they get, you know, extra sparkly. Then we all hide in the grass and wait for the horn to come to the beach."

Comet whooped and floated, yelling "Best sleepover ever!" again and again.

When Comet calmed down, Twilight finally said, "Okay, I'll do it, but you guys have to promise to stay close by. Also, where are we going to find the sparkly stuff?"

Shamrock's heart leapt right out of his chest. "The CAVES!" he blurted out.

His friends just stared at him.

Shamrock shook his shoulders, straightened his glasses, and tried to get back some scientific seriousness. "Ahem, I mean, there are sparkly rocks in the caves, remember? Perhaps we could gather those."

"Great idea!" Sapphire replied. "I've seen them before, and I think they're sparkly enough to lure the ghost."

"If you guys don't mind, I'm going to skip the caves. I have a surprise for all of us," Comet said with a wiggle of her eyebrows.

"Do you need any help?" Twilight asked.

"Actually, yeah!" Comet said. "That would be great."

The two of them huddled together and made plans during the rest of the way back.

Shamrock and Sapphire walked in silence, as they did quite a lot when they were at Unicorn University. They were both thinkers. Shamrock was usually thinking about a book he had just read, and Sapphire was usually dreaming about where she'd like to travel when she got older.

Shamrock thought that perhaps Comet's surprise would be some sort of baked treat, and he was very much looking forward to it. He was also pleased that he was going to explore the caves sooner than he'd thought he would. Maybe he could go with the flow a little bit more. Maybe.

Shamrock and Sapphire peeled off from Twilight and Comet at the barn and made their way to the beach. On the walk, Shamrock noticed something—or a few somethings—dashing in and out of the grass. He could tell it wasn't the wind, but the little creatures were too quick to see.

"What's that in the grass, Sapphire?" he asked.

"They're ghosts!" Sapphire shouted, making Shamrock almost jump out of his coat. From her *shout*—not because of "ghosts," he assured himself.

Sapphire laughed and nudged him with her flank. Shamrock giggled, but he did wonder if he might have been more affected by all this ghost talk than he'd realized.

"No, not really," Sapphire explained. "They're sand pixies of course."

Shamrock nodded. "Oh, I see! We have grass pixies in the mountains, and they make the same sounds. I've never been able to see one up close, but I've read about them. What about you?"

"Yeah, they're too quick to see. Hmm. You know, I've read about ghosts, too, and now I've seen one!"

Shamrock just shook his head. He could see the caves up ahead and raced toward them. Sapphire followed closely behind.

They both paused at the mouth of the cave and stared in wonder at the sparkling rocks. The sun was shining into the cave, making the floor and walls glimmer and shine like diamonds. Shamrock felt like they had found the treasure without the help of any ghost.

6

To Catch a Ghost

After dinner, Shamrock led the way toward the beach. He couldn't wait to conduct the experiment and prove that his hypothesis was right and the others were wrong. He whistled and swished his tail as he pranced through the grass.

Everyone settled at the spot where Sapphire had first glimpsed the ghost.

"Okay!" Sapphire yelled out in her best organizing voice. "Everyone, get some driftwood for the fire, and pile it here." She pointed with her horn to the small hole she'd dug in the sand.

When they'd gathered enough wood, Sapphire arranged

the pile and made a campfire. Shamrock remembered when she'd learned to do that at school from one of the chefs, Stella. Stella was a dragon and knew tons about fire.

"Shamrock, do you have the sparkling rocks?" Sapphire asked.

He sure did. Shamrock had loved gathering the rocks and was excited to bring them home after all this. Some were huge and white with silver specks, and some were shining gray. A few even had purple streaked through them. He handed the bag to Twilight just before she used her special ability to become invisible. Shamrock, Sapphire, and Comet hid in the tall grasses off to the side. They peered through dark green strands to see Twilight line the rocks up in front of the fire so they would sparkle in the light.

"Beautiful!" Sapphire said with awe.

Everyone nodded as they watched the rocks shimmer. Twilight crept back to the grass and dropped her invisibility.

"Now what?" Comet asked.

"Now we wait," Sapphire told her, and crouched a little lower behind the grass.

Shamrock looked up to see the many constellations in the sky. It was such a clear night, he didn't even need a telescope.

"There's the Big Horn," he pointed out, looking up to the constellation that looked like a triangle made of big, bright stars.

Comet laughed. "At first I thought you meant the ghost was here."

Shamrock laughed too. He could understand the mistake.

"Shh, don't scare the ghost," Sapphire reminded them.

"This is pretty cool, though. I read all about the constellations over break," Shamrock said very quietly. "See the tip of the horn? The very brightest star?"

Comet nodded.

"That points north, and unicorns have used it forever to guide their way. There are lots of stories about it."

"Kind of reminds me of what Uncle Sea Star said earlier," Twilight whispered. Shamrock didn't see the connection between ghosts and stars but decided not to say anything. He didn't want to hurt Twilight's feelings.

"Guys, focus on the water!" Sapphire whisper-yelled. "We don't want to miss the Glowing Horn."

They did focus on the ocean, but still no ghost appeared. Soon their legs were cramped, and they all started fidgeting in the grass.

"Maybe the ghost wasn't real, after all," Sapphire said with disappointment.

"Maybe it's just feeling shy," Twilight told her. They all knew Twilight understood that feeling.

"Maybe you were right, Shamrock," Comet sighed. She walked over to the fire and flopped dramatically onto the sand. "All this for nothing!"

"No way! Not for nothing!" Shamrock shouted. He felt like he had taken a big gulp of warm cider, and he was filled with a warm glow from head to toe. He jumped up with glee and raised his horn high into the air as he trotted around the fire. "The experiment proved that I was right! I told you guys all day. I told you! I'm taking a mental picture of this moment right now."

His glasses had gone askew in his excitement, and he

shook his head back to straighten them. Using his special ability, he filed away a memory movie of the moment.

"Well, I still have my surprise!" Comet said, ignoring his speech. She scooted over a large black skillet of cupcakes she had brought and put it by the fire. "Just to warm them up a little," she explained.

Soon the smell of freshly baked cupcakes filled the air, and it wasn't just Shamrock who was feeling good. *Freshly baked cupcakes, I'm surrounded by my best friends, and I was totally proved right. This might be the best picnic ever,* Shamrock thought.

He smiled and looked out at the dark ocean, and then, all of a sudden, he could see the impossible. His jaw dropped when he saw a Glowing Horn emerge from the ocean and float toward them.

7

Running from Ghosts!

G host!" Shamrock shrieked.

"Come on, Shamrock," Sapphire groaned. "We get it! Stop being mean."

"Yeah, ha ha." Comet rolled her eyes.

"No, no, look, look!" Shamrock said. His eyes felt like they were about to pop through his glasses. "The horn is—"

Twilight looked up to see what Shamrock was pointing at. "Coming right at us!" Twilight squeaked.

"Better get moving!" Sapphire shouted when she saw it too.

No one needed to be told twice. Shamrock scrambled up from the sand to run with his friends back to their tent, leaving the cupcakes and rock treasures for the ghost.

"Didn't we *want* to find the ghost?" Comet, almost out of breath, reminded them as she ran.

"I guess we didn't think about the fact that scary ghosts are, well, scary! So we gotta run faster!" Twilight yelled louder than any of them had heard her yell before.

When they got to the tent, they turned back to see the Glowing Horn still glimmering over the surface of the ocean. Shamrock looked at the tent and felt way too scared to sleep outside.

"Um," Shamrock ventured in a shaky voice, "maybe we sleep in your room tonight?"

"Totally," Sapphire agreed without even pausing to think. They all grabbed their bags and made their way into the big red barn.

Soon they were settled in Sapphire's room—snuggled close together with the lights on—but they couldn't stop thinking about the ghost. Shamrock could feel his friends shivering beside him. Of course, they had wanted to see it, but now they'd didn't remember why! What if the ghost was mad that they tried to trick it? Shamrock took a deep breath to calm down and think rationally. But what was rational about a ghost?

"I don't think I can sleep tonight," Twilight admitted. "We just saw a ghost! And it's still out there!"

"I'm sorry about earlier, guys," Shamrock told them. "I was not being a good friend at all. You were right, and I was so, so, so very wrong."

Comet waved her hoof as if to shoo away the apology. "Honestly, I thought this was just a fun game. I am

as surprised as you are that we saw a ghost!"

"Me too! I am surprised our trap worked," Twilight admitted. "I was only going along with it because I didn't think the ghost was actually going to visit."

"Me too," Sapphire agreed. "I mean, I really did think I saw the ghost at first, but as the day went on, I kinda thought I'd imagined it."

Everyone started laughing at once. Turned out Shamrock wasn't the only one to think the ghost wasn't real, after all! Their laughter broke the tension, and soon enough everyone was able to settle down to sleep.

Shamrock felt a little silly for being so serious about the ghost all day. His friends had just been having fun!

He lay awake longer than the others, not sure what to think about laying eyes on a ghostly being. What did it mean to have Uncle Sea Star's story be real? Had he been telling the truth about other things too? It all made Shamrock's head spin. Eventually, when his head was too full of questions for him to think anymore, Shamrock finally drifted off to sleep.

8

Sweet Discovery

Everything was different in the bright morning sunshine. As he sat up and yawned, Shamrock regretted being scared of the Glowing Horn. And now they had lost their chance to talk to a ghost. *A missed scientific opportunity!*

Shamrock, Comet, Twilight, and Sapphire ate breakfast at their tent that morning. Everyone agreed with Shamrock, that they were silly to have been afraid the night before.

"It's not like it was being mean or anything," Twilight pointed out.

"If anything, it was friendly! Coming over to say hello," Comet added.

Sapphire shook her head. "I can't believe we were all so scared. We totally missed our chance."

"I don't know about that," Shamrock pushed back. He suddenly had a fluttering feeling. An idea was taking shape!

"But our parents are coming to pick us up this afternoon," Twilight said.

"Yeah, we don't have another night to look for the ghost," said Comet.

Shamrock just smiled. "But we don't need to wait for nighttime. Remember, Sapphire first saw the Glowing Horn during the day. Most might think a ghost will only appear at night, but we know that's not true in this case. Even though we're dealing with the supernatural, we can still approach this situation rationally. Now, what else do we know about this ghost?"

Sapphire was nodding enthusiastically. This was the type of adventure she was looking for. "Great thinking, Shamrock. We know the ghost appeared when we put the shining rocks out, like Uncle Sea Star said it would."

"No, wait!" Comet said. "The ghost totally came for

my cupcakes, remember? I mean, they *are* good. You know, I created the recipe myself. My great-aunt had a certain version, but she didn't use cinnamon—"

Shamrock's horn went into the air with a start. "And before that, it came out when we were having a picnic!"

"You're right!" Twilight agreed. "This ghost is hungry."

"And has a sweet tooth," Shamrock added.

"I like this ghost. And I even have more cupcakes!" Comet said. They didn't need treasure or sparkly things to talk with the ghost. They needed sugar!

"Okay, okay," Sapphire said to get the group's attention. "But what will we do this time if the ghost does come back?"

"Not run away," Comet said.

Sapphire laughed. "Yeah, but how do we get it to tell us where the treasure is?"

"I think we should record the sights, sounds, and movements of this ghost," Shamrock was quick to say. "This is quite a major discovery, and we must act like scientists. I mean, we could be interviewed for a book—"

"Personally, I prefer to act like a treasure hunter," Comet interrupted.

"Either way, let's just be nice to this ghost, and hopefully we'll learn lots of different things," Twilight said.

"As always, Twilight knows exactly what to say!" Sapphire said. Everyone laughed. They all knew that when Twilight said something, it was worth saying.

The four friends agreed to be nice and welcoming to the Glowing Horn. No one wanted to upset a ghost!

9

The Sweet Tooth

Like his friends, Shamrock carried sweets in a basket down to the beach. Not only did they bring Comet's famous cupcakes but they found cookies and seaweed muffins as well. They wanted to bring a feast to tempt the ghost!

Shamrock's heart fluttered with excitement. He couldn't believe how wrong he'd been earlier. This was quite the scientific discovery. He thought more about what it would be like to be interviewed. Maybe they would meet a famous writer. Or maybe they would write their own book and become famous themselves! He was kicking himself for not using his ability last night. He had only recently discovered that he had a superpowered photographic memory that could take memory movies of what he saw. He could even access other people's memories if he tried hard enough. He would have to remember to ask his friends to describe their own experiences with the ghost to him in detail later.

Down at the beach, the four unicorns laid a blanket down and piled all their treats together. Twilight, always the most artistic in the group, made sure to arrange things so they looked as beautiful as possible.

Everyone waited quietly. At first nothing happened, and Comet started shifting on her hooves, impatient to see the ghost again. Then Shamrock remembered they had been yelling about a muffin break when Sapphire had first seen the ghost.

"Wow, look at all these amazing sweets!" Shamrock shouted at the ocean.

Comet picked up on his thoughts immediately. "Wow,

so many delicious things to eat!" she shouted.

"Never seen so many amazing sweets!" Shamrock yelled.

The four friends wiggled on their hooves and tried not to giggle as they waited. Each looked in a different direction so as not to miss the ghost, and they continued yelling about their sugary picnic.

After what seemed like a long time but was perhaps just a few minutes, the Glowing Horn was back. And floating toward them!

This time the friends stood their ground. They were going to talk to the Glowing Horn.

"Steady, unicorns, steady," Sapphire reminded them. "We are going to stay here and welcome the ghost."

Shamrock felt his heart beating inside his chest as he watched the Glowing Horn get bigger and bigger as it rose out of the ocean. Even though they had decided not to be afraid of the ghost, Shamrock couldn't help but be a little frighted.

The Glowing Horn was becoming much bigger than your average unicorn horn as it moved toward them. And it had that special glow, more like the stars on Shamrock's backpack than the glitter of their own horns. Even in bright sunshine, they could see it glow!

Then, suddenly, Shamrock realized it wasn't a ghost at all.

10

A New Friend

The creature's head broke through the water, revealing the smile of the young blue narwhal floating toward them. "Hey, guys, do you think I could have a cupcake? All I've had is seaweed for *weeks*!"

All four unicorns just stared back in surprise.

"I'm Ned, by the way," the young narwhal said. He raised his eyebrows when the unicorns still didn't say anything back.

Shamrock was the first to find his words. "Hi, I'm Shamrock. Are you a narwhal? We thought you were the Glowing Horn ghost! But it's strange, right? For a narwhal to be in these warm waters? Are you lost? And your horn is

glowing! I've never read anything about narwhals having glowing horns." All his thoughts spilled out so fast, he could hardly breathe. Having grown up in the mountains, Shamrock had never met a narwhal before. Of course, he'd read a ton about them. *1,000 Incredible and Astonishing Facts* even had a whole page about how a narwhal horn could grow up to ten feet long. As always when he met someone new, Shamrock found himself babbling and spurting out facts. It reminded him of when he had met Twilight on their very first day of school.

Ned just laughed at all his questions. "No way! I mean, yeah, I'm a narwhal. But I'm not lost. I'm on vacation with my family. My horn is glowing 'cause of the special water in the hidden caves, you know?"

The four unicorns just blinked at him for a beat.

Then Sapphire finally said, "I've lived by this beach

my whole life, and I've never seen a narwhal around here! And I've never heard of hidden caves." She shook her head. Shamrock thought she would have been less surprised if she really had been talking to a ghost.

Ned laughed again. He smiled as he bobbed a little in the water. "Well, we usually stick to the deeper caves and don't come up here, because the water is so warm and we like the cold. But I kept smelling and hearing about all these sweets, and we've had to eat boring seaweed for weeks now. And, well, I had to see if I could have some treats."

"Totally!" Comet said, sounding like her old self again. "I baked these myself. Cinnamon is the trick to the recipe."

Comet waved at the blanket with her horn, and Shamrock wondered how Ned was supposed to get a cupcake. *He can't walk on sand, right?* Shamrock wondered before shaking his head. *Of course he can't! Be rational. Get a hold of yourself!*

"I think you'll need to toss him one," Shamrock told Comet when he'd cleared his thoughts.

"Would you mind?" Ned asked a little sheepishly. "They do smell good."

Comet tossed him two cupcakes in a row, and Ned caught them both in his mouth and swallowed them whole.

Shamrock started to wonder about the hidden caves. That really would be a scientific discovery for unicorns! He hadn't read about them in any of his books.

"Um, could you tell us about the hidden caves?" Shamrock asked, after Ned had eaten another four cupcakes.

"Actually, I might be able to show you. It's super cool. Everything glows and stuff," Ned told him, his mouth still full. "But I think you'll need a boat. Unicorns can't swim that far, right?"

"No, not as far as narwhals anyway," Sapphire admitted. "Luckily, we do know someone with a boat."

Shamrock looked up to see Uncle Sea Star's boat coming toward them. Somehow Sapphire's uncle always arrived just in time. Shamrock smiled. He was starting to sound like one of the sea legends.

"Ahoy there!" Uncle Sea Star called to them. "A narwhal

in Sunshine Springs? Well, I never heard of such a thing! Captain Sea Star at your service," he said, bowing his head.

"I'm Ned! I was going to show my new friends the glowing caves. Care to give them a lift?"

Of course, Uncle Sea Star was always up for such an adventure. The five unicorns sailed after Ned as he led them farther out into the water. He stopped short in what seemed like the middle of the ocean, and Shamrock wondered what kind of special powers he had to make him see what unicorns could not. But Uncle Sea Star dropped the anchor, and the unicorns jumped into the ocean and swam after Ned. The entrance to the cave wasn't too deep, and they just had to make a quick right before they popped up in a glowing dome filled with natural beauty.

At first Shamrock's glasses were all fogged up from the swim, and he could only see the strange light coming off the walls. When the lenses finally cleared up, he looked around to see his friends talking with other narwhals and exploring the caves. Big rocks gleamed in bright oranges, reds, and purples all over the cave, and strange, friendly fish swam around them. He could see Comet teaching a younger nar-whal how to high-U, and Sapphire had her serious face on as she listened to an older narwhal tell her the history of the caves.

Shamrock watched a little glowing, spotted fish use its suction-cup hands to climb out of the water and up the walls of the cave. Miraculously, the same fish flapped its fins to fly through a curtain of glowing vines. Shamrock felt like he was dreaming.

Twilight walked over to him with glitter on her nose. "I've been studying that extra sparkly wall over there," she explained. "I think I'd like to paint a picture of this to remember it all by. Since not all of us have a special photo-graphic memory." She smiled and gave him a little nudge.

Shamrock smiled too. "We really have made an incredible discovery today. It's not even included in *1,000 Incredible and Astonishing Facts*!"

Twilight scrunched her nose and tilted her head. "But we didn't discover this, Shamrock. The ghost story of the Glowing Horn means that unicorns have known about these caves forever. Not to mention how long the narwhals have known about them."

Shamrock was speechless for a moment. Suddenly Uncle Sea Star's words made sense to him. There is truth to the sea legends, even when they seem very untrue! By playing and experimenting with his friends, Shamrock had learned more today than if he had convinced them all to stick to his careful plans. Plus, they had made so many new friends. For a while, Shamrock could only stare at Twilight in wonder, his jaw just hanging open. He shook his head to gain some composure.

"The Glowing Horn brought us to the secret treasure after all!" Shamrock shouted. His old friends and his new friends looked over at him from around the cave and smiled. "Hear, hear!" Uncle Sea Star cheered back.

Shamrock felt like the luckiest unicorn in the universe.

Comet's Big Win

1

Apple-Oat Muffins
with Sugar Crystals

Comet couldn't believe her eyes. Unicorn University had been totally transformed!

Today was the school's club fair, and there were tents with waving flags, horns trumpeting joyful music, and cheerful chatter all around her. It looked like a carnival she'd gone to when she was little, but instead of circus performers there were students everywhere. The dance club was performing onstage. The science club was bubbling up purple slime at a booth. There was even a juggling club balancing plates on their horns. All the activity made Comet smile.

Growing up in a large family, Comet had always felt more at home in big, noisy crowds. She felt like she could wander around all day.

Comet soon spotted her three very best friends huddled together over by the gardening club's table. Plants of every color and shape were piled so high, you could hardly see the unicorns in the booth behind them. Shamrock, a mint-colored unicorn with huge, black-rimmed glasses, seemed to be studying a large piece of paper. Twilight, who stood out with her jet-black coat and brightly painted hooves, was looking all around her, clearly distracted by everything that was going on. And Sapphire, a blue unicorn with long braids, was pointing to something on Shamrock's paper with her horn. Comet was sure they were deciding which booth to check out next.

I have to tell them about the baking booth! she remembered. The school's chefs, Stella and Celest, had told her a secret: the first students to get to the baking club booth would get a special treat! And no one made treats like Stella and Celest. The fair was already in full swing, and Comet knew that she and her friends had to get to the baking booth fast. She started running over, but—oh no!—she got a little too excited and her special flying power kicked in. Soon Comet was a rose-colored blur speeding right toward her friends, and with a crash, she knocked them over like bowling pins.

Comet untangled herself from the group while shouting funny apologies. A couple of other unicorns grumbled about the mess, but most unicorns were used to Comet's dramatic entrances. She was still adjusting to her magical ability and was always flying into things or accidently floating away.

Comet and her friends got to their hooves, laughing as the dust settled.

"We were actually just looking for you, Comet," said Twilight.

"Yeah, we were trying to figure out which booth we should check out," Shamrock told her. His glasses had gone crooked in the fall, so he shook his head to straighten them.

"But don't worry, Comet. I already told them you couldn't join any clubs during hoofball season," Sapphire added. She said it matter-of-factly, as if she and Comet had already discussed it.

Comet felt like she had fallen down all over again. *No clubs?!* "What do you mean?" she asked.

"Comet!" Sapphire blew out her lips, giving her friend a look. "Coach told us last week! Everyone on the hoofball team has to be ready for the big game against Glitterhorn College. Which of course means focusing on practice. And nothing else!"

Comet laughed, tossing her bangs out of her eyes. "Oh, come on, Sapphire! We are never going to play in that game. We'll just be there in case, like, *all* the other players get hurt. We're only first years!"

Sapphire shook her head and looked determined. "No way! Coach said we could play if we worked really hard."

Comet just shrugged. They didn't have time to get into this when they really needed to score one of Stella and Celest's surprise treats. "We're wasting time, guys! We have to make it to the baking booth!" Comet broke into a brisk trot before there could be anymore hoofball talk. Sapphire had gotten really into hoofball lately and wanted Comet to be as serious as she was. Comet liked running around on the field with her friends, but she didn't really know why the match against Glitterhorn College was such a big deal.

Sapphire, Shamrock, and Twilight caught up with Comet at the baking booth. She was already munching on an apple-oat muffin sprinkled with crunchy sugar crystals.

"Don't tell anyone, but we saved some muffins for you four!" Stella said, handing them each a sugary treat from a basket stashed under the table. Stella was a dragon with beautiful green scales that sparkled in the afternoon sun.

Celest laughed. "Well, you just said that so loudly, you told everyone yourself!" Celest was a gray speckled unicorn, and the other chef at the school. She and Stella led the baking club every year, in addition to feeding the whole school.

Stella groaned. "Oh, come on. I'm just excited about these award-winning muffins!"

"So, are you guys signing up for the baking club?" Celest asked them. "It's going to be so fun!"

"Sorry, Celest. I've decided on the astronomy club," Shamrock told her. "I was thinking about the science club, but I think I can only do one thing this year."

"Same," Twilight agreed. "I'm going for the art club. Our first project is sculpting! I've never done that before."

"See, Comet?" Sapphire said. "Most unicorns sign up for only one thing. And you already signed up for hoofball."

"Well, I am not your average unicorn!" Comet said. "Where's that baking club sign-up sheet?"

Celest pushed a clipboard her way. "I hope we can handle you, Comet!"

"You probably can't," Comet said, trying to keep a straight face.

Comet looked up from the clipboard to see Sapphire's most serious face staring right at her.

"Comet, this hoofball game is a big deal. Coach is counting on us!" Sapphire told her.

Comet could see how worried her friend was, and was quick to make her feel better. "Really, I can handle both. I'm always sneaking off to the kitchens. This won't be any different!"

Sapphire smiled. "Promise?"

"Super promise with peppermint whipped cream on top," Comet said, giving Sapphire a horn tap.

2

Orange Slices with Cinnamon

The next day, Sapphire and Comet walked toward the field for hoofball practice. The air was crisp and cool, and all the leaves had turned from green to bright oranges, reds, and yellows. Comet watched the swirling leaves whip up and around in the wind, and felt the call of her own hooves wanting to fly up with them. She shook her head and stared at the grass, trying to ground herself. She didn't want to go flying into the whole hoofball team!

"Hey, Comet. Look, here comes Flash," Sapphire pointed out.

Flash was the captain of the hoofball team, and Comet and Sapphire agreed that she was the coolest unicorn at Unicorn University. She tied back her rainbow mane with a purple bandanna and always wore sparkly blue eyeliner, even to practice. Plus, she was the best player on the team. Flash could pull off this awesome spin-and-kick move that no one else would even try. Everyone on the team looked up to her.

"Hey, Saph! Com!" Flash greeted them. She had a bag of hoofballs slung around her neck. "Ready for practice?"

"Totally!" Sapphire squeaked. "We can't wait to win against Glitterhorn!"

"Awesome!" Flash cheered. "Hey, I'd better get going. I told Coach I'd help her set up for practice. See you guys soon!"

Flash broke into a gallop and ran up ahead of them. She was also the fastest unicorn in the school, so it wasn't long before she was out of sight.

"Can you believe it?" Sapphire asked.

"Flash totally talked to us! And she gave us *nicknames*," Comet said.

Sapphire and Comet chatted about their good luck all the way to the field, and stopped only when Coach's sharp whistle blew to gather the team together before practice.

Comet smelled the grass and dirt that got kicked up as the team huddled together, and she smiled as the cool breeze brushed the side of her cheek.

"Okay, team!" Coach boomed so that everyone could hear. "As you all know, the big game is just two weeks away, and we need to get ready. Today we're going to focus on our magical strategies. So, who can remind everyone of the rules about magical abilities?"

"You can use your magic for only thirty seconds at a time, so make sure to have a plan," Flash said.

"Can you give us an example?" Coach asked.

"Well, I can change my appearance, you know? Sometimes

it helps for me to distract the other team by flashing different colors. Just to get a little advantage. You have to work with what you've got."

"Precisely. Let's break into twos. Think about how your abilities could help you in the game," Coach told them.

The team broke up into pairs and spread out over the field.

As usual, Comet and Sapphire found their favorite spot by the bleachers.

"You know, you have the best ability for hoofball, Comet," Sapphire said.

Comet laughed. "No way! Remember yesterday when I knocked everyone over? What would happen if I did that during a game?"

"If you knocked over the *other* team, it would be great!" Sapphire smiled. "I mean it, though. Like, what if I kicked the ball up to you? You can totally control your floating now."

Comet thought about it. She *had* gotten better at floating above the ground. Just as long as she didn't fly up too high and didn't move too much. Sapphire usually had good ideas, so Comet always trusted her vision. And Sapphire had a great kick. She could always make the hoofball do exactly what she wanted. "Okay, let's try it!" Comet ran down the field a little and hovered above the ground. "Go for it!"

Sapphire kicked the ball into the air so that it went right by Comet's front left hoof. Comet got to it just in time and sent it soaring across the field all the way to the goal!

"Comet! You scored!" Sapphire cheered.

"No, *we* scored!" Comet called back.

The two friends jumped up and down, cheering "We scored! We scored!" until Coach told them to settle down and get focused on practice.

After running some other drills, Coach blew the whistle to signal the end of practice.

Time for my favorite part! Comet thought as she saw Flash carrying a tray filled with orange slices sprinkled with cinnamon. Comet zoned out as her mind drifted to thoughts of baking. *Maybe I'll try to make an orange-and-cinnamon cake, or even ice cream! I'll have to ask Stella if—*

"Comet, listen!" Sapphire hissed. Comet looked up to see Coach speaking to the team about extra hoofball practices.

"Oops, sorry!" Comet whispered.

3

Breakfast Biscuits

The next morning, Comet work up early. She was meeting the baking club so they could make a breakfast feast together before classes started. Comet couldn't think of a better way to start the day.

The stables were still cold in the early morning air, so she pulled her cozy blanket around her shoulders and left her stall. The snores and sighs of her classmates surrounded her as she crept quietly outside.

Even the sun was still waking up, peeking over the rolling hills and filling the sky with bright orange-and-pink light. Comet's breath created little clouds as she made her way to the kitchens.

Soon she could see friendly smoke blooming from the crooked stone chimney, and the glow of a cozy fire through the big kitchen window. Comet trotted the rest of the way, eager to get started.

A few other unicorns arrived at the kitchens just as Comet did.

"Hey, Storm!" Comet called to her classmate, a three-legged gray unicorn.

"Mornin'," Storm mumbled as she shuffled toward the door. She looked half-asleep.

Stella ushered everyone into the kitchen. The big wooden table had five baking stations set up. Each place had a mixing bowl, two eggs, a measuring cup filled with flour, a glass of milk, a stick of butter, and a kitchen towel. And a horn-written recipe next to each place.

Comet took her spot by two unicorns with matching

gold heart charms hanging from their necks.

"Hi, I'm Glinda! And this is Spark," the unicorn closest to her said, her charm wiggling as she pointed to the bright purple unicorn beside her.

"Hey. I'm Comet! I just love your charms."

"They're friendship charms!" Spark told her.

Comet was about to ask her more about them, but Stella was starting class. "Good morning! Take your places, everyone!" she said, gesturing with her long, flour-covered claws.

"Today we're making biscuits. Let's start by studying the recipe," Celest added. She and Stella wore matching white aprons, not that the fabric had done much to keep them free of flour dust. Stella had a streak of flour over her eye, and Celest's usually glittering horn was totally covered.

The class got to work reading their recipe cards. Once everyone had looked over the measurements and instructions, the kitchen soon filled with laughter and the comforting sounds of bowls clanging together. Comet had made

biscuits lots of times, but they'd always turned out a little dry. Not like the fluffy ones Stella and Celest made. She was excited to learn their secret.

It wasn't long before Comet was in the baking zone. The smells of the kitchen always grounded her. Her hooves weren't trying to fly away, because they were right where they wanted to be. When she spotted the bowl of oranges on the counter, Comet had an idea. She crept over to the counter and grabbed a few from the bowl, along with another special ingredient. Her biscuits were going to be *awesome*. Or at least she hoped!

Comet could feel her heart flutter as she pushed her tray of biscuits into the oven. She tried to keep the smile off her face as, through the oven window, she watched the dough rise. She had a feeling these would wow the club.

Soon everyone's biscuits were pulled from the oven and the club members displayed their fluffy creations on the big wooden table. Everyone went around and tasted what each unicorn had made. Comet wasn't the only one who'd added a special twist.

Stormy laughed when Spark asked her why she'd added candy to her breakfast. "Because chocolate makes everything better!"

Glinda blew out her cheeks as she looked at her own biscuits. They had all somehow melted down into a sludge that covered the baking sheet. "Even chocolate couldn't have saved these," she groaned.

"Wow, Comet! These are the best biscuits I've ever had," said Stormy after wandering over to Comet's station. "Where did you get the idea for the orange-and-cinnamon flavor?"

"Hoofball!" Comet cheered. Stormy just raised her eyebrows.

"Okay, bakers!" Stella called, quieting the club. "It's time for you to get to class. See you next week, same time and place!"

Comet had study hall in the library as her first class of the day, so she hung back to help with cleanup. It looked like a sugary explosion in the kitchen.

"You know, your biscuits really were spectacular, Comet," Stella said as they wiped down the table.

Comet blushed. "I just added a little extra spice. I saw it on the counter and felt like it would be the perfect thing!"

"A true baker!" Celest said. "You listened to the ingredients. You know, you should enter the baking competition against Glitterhorn in a couple of weeks. It's right after the hoofball match."

"That's true!" Stella

agreed. "You're always surprising me with your baking, Comet."

"It's not as big a deal as the hoofball match, of course," Celest added quickly.

Stella laughed. "Only the baking club shows up at the tent to watch. I guess baking is not quite as exciting as hoofball."

Comet didn't agree. She loved reading cookbooks, and being in the kitchen was just as fun as being on the hoofball field. And even though she could hear Sapphire's objections already, she couldn't help but be interested in the idea of baking in the competition.

"If you win, you get to compete in the Five Kingdoms Bakeoff, against kids from all over the world! Which is better than a trophy, I think," Celest said.

"And you get to bring friends. Every baker goes with a team of three others. I have a feeling I know some unicorns who would like to travel to the competition with you. It's in a new place every year," Stella added.

"We could set up some extra lessons to help you get ready! That would be fun. I really think you could be our best shot at winning. Truth be told, we usually lose," Celest said.

"Wow, I would love to," Comet told them, feeling her cheeks heat up. No one had ever said she was the best before. Maybe the silliest. But never the best. She felt as warm as her freshly baked biscuits.

4

The Secret Ingredient

omet was so excited, she half walked, half floated out
of the kitchens. She wondered what a baking competition would be like. Comet had always loved baking for
her friends and for her family, but no one had ever taken her
passion so seriously before. It was an amazing feeling.

As she made her way across the lawn, she was surprised
to see Sapphire, practically floating herself.

Uh-oh. Comet suddenly felt flatter than a pancake. *What
will she think of the baking competition?*

"Comet!" Sapphire yelled, running over when she saw

her friend. "You won't believe what happened! Coach told me the best news."

Comet smiled at Sapphire's good mood. Maybe this would all work out! "No way! Because I just got glitter-tastic news too!"

"Me first," Sapphire said. "Coach and Flash saw our move yesterday, the one where I kick and you float? And they want us to do it in the game. Coach called us the secret ingredient. I'm so excited. They're going to add extra prac-tices just for us!" The words rushed out of her, like she couldn't tell her friend fast enough.

Comet couldn't help but smile, seeing Sapphire so excited. "Wow, Sapphire!"

"Baking club won't mess with practices, right?" Sapphire asked. "Remember you promised!"

Comet's heart skipped a beat. How could she tell Sapphire about the baking competition now? She didn't want to break a promise.

"I mean, you don't really need me for the special move," Comet told her, biting her bottom lip. "It's all about your perfect kick!"

Sapphire smiled. "No way! We're a team! I totally need you."

Comet didn't know what to say. She didn't want to let Sapphire down. Maybe she could do both things? *The competition is after the hoofball match,* she thought. *I can totally pull this off! Easy peasy.* Comet puffed herself up like a soufflé fresh out of the oven.

"Actually, you're right! This is great!" Comet told her. "Does this mean we get to hang out with Flash?"

She thought about telling Sapphire that she was also going to enter the baking competition, but she couldn't quite get the words out before Sapphire said, "Yes! And it's super rare for first years to play in the Glitterhorn game. Our name could be on a trophy!"

Comet laughed as Sapphire sang, "We're going to get a trophy! We're going to get a trophy!" all the way to their first classes of the day.

But Comet couldn't quite shake the feeling that she had done something wrong. *Should I have told her about the baking contest?* she thought as she trailed behind Sapphire. *Oh, but she would just worry. And that would distract her from the big game!* After quite a bit of back-and-forth with

herself, Comet decided that the best thing was to keep the baking competition a secret. Then no one would worry and everyone would be happily surprised when she won! Really, what could go wrong?

5

A Cup of Tea and a Cookie

The next week flew by. Comet had been so busy with all the extra practices that she could hardly believe the Glitterhorn competitions were now only a week away.

"You know, Comet, I think I'm going to start calling you 'the Blur,'" Twilight said as Comet grabbed an apple from their lunch tree.

"What do you mean?" Comet asked with her mouth full. She had time for only a quick break before rushing off to baking practice, but she had promised Twilight they would have lunch together. Comet was starting to think she should stop making promises altogether.

"You're always running from one place to the next," Twilight told her. "I never see you anymore. Is everything okay?"

Comet rolled her eyes. "Of course! Just, you know, busy."

"Okay—" Twilight started, but Comet didn't let her finish.

"I'm sorry, but I gotta go!" Comet said, partly so she wouldn't be late and partly because she knew that if they kept talking, she would let her big secret slip. Comet had stuck to her plan, and only the baking club knew she was training for the baking competition. Comet told herself she was keeping a secret because she didn't want anyone to worry about her, but when she looked back at Twilight's crestfallen face, she wondered if she was doing the right thing.

After a brisk gallop, Comet pushed open the big wooden door to the kitchen, and stifled her yawn when she saw Stella coming toward her with an apron. Comet didn't want her to know how tired she was. Stella and Celest were helping her so much, and on top of their job of feeding the school! She didn't want to let them down.

"Good afternoon, Comet," Celest said from across the room. She peered over her wire-rimmed reading glasses. A gigantic cookbook was open in front of her.

Comet smiled when she saw all the little handwritten notes in the margins and the food splotches that stained the old pages. There was something about old cookbooks that Comet had always loved. They made her feel like she was connected to generations of bakers.

"What's that for?" she asked, pointing to the cookbook with her horn.

"To help you find your special cake recipe, of course," Stella said.

Comet blinked, confused for a moment. "Oh! The one I'll bake at the competition?"

"Have you thought of any ideas, dear?" Celest added,

clearly trying to hide the concern in her voice. "We have only a week to prepare, after all."

Comet blushed, her already pink cheeks turning a deep shade of red. "Um—I meant to last night before bed but, well, I fell asleep." She felt like she'd burned their batch of chocolate chip cookies. The truth was that she had lain awake thinking about possible recipes, but nothing seemed good enough. The whole baking club was so excited for her. What if she wasn't as good a baker as they thought?

"Why don't you look through this book now? We can take a break from practicing, and I'll make you a cup of tea," Celest told her kindly.

Comet felt her whole body relax at the idea. A quiet minute alone with a cookbook? She almost cried with relief. "Thank you so much."

When she was all settled by the book with her cup of tea and a cinnamon sugar cookie, she began to study recipes from all over the five kingdoms. She couldn't believe how

many different types of cakes there were. Some sounded amazing, like the triple chocolate cake with chocolate whipped cream, and some sounded not so good, like prune cake with candied twigs. She searched for one to make for the competition. She had to choose a cake that best represented her school. Which seemed impossible. There were so many different parts of Unicorn University! How could one cake represent everyone? And, the worst thought of all, what if it turned out wrong?

Comet tried to shake her doubts off and kept turning the weathered pages. There was still plenty of time to figure it out. Right?

6

A Lump of
Uncooked Dough

"Comet? Comet! Wake up!"

"Huh? Where am I?" Comet whipped her head around and accidently knocked over a stack of books. The pile of cookbooks she had meant to look through all tumbled to the floor, making the whole library turn and say, "Shush!"

"You're in a library, not a barn!" a unicorn at the table next to them said. Comet could only see a sparkling horn above that unicorn's own stack of books.

"Sorry," Comet whispered. She glanced at Shamrock.

His bushy eyebrows were furrowed over his glasses. He seemed worried. "Comet, are you okay?"

Comet felt her jaw set. She was so sick of people asking her that. She'd been practicing for the baking competition and the hoofball match for the past two weeks, and, sure, she was tired. But she was more tired of Shamrock and Twilight giving her sad looks and asking how she was all the time. The competitions with Glitterhorn were the next day. Couldn't everyone leave her alone until everything was all over?

"ARGH! Shamrock, if you ask me that one more time, I swear I'm going to . . . I'm going to . . ." Comet huffed. "I will be super mad at you!"

Shamrock frowned. "It's just that you keep falling asleep. I mean, we were in the middle of a conversation, and then—poof!—you nodded off. Again."

Comet sighed. That *was* pretty rude of her. "I'm sorry. I only have to get through tomorrow, and then I'll be back to normal."

"Is it all the extra hoofball practice?"

"And all the baking—" Comet stopped short, because just then a couple of older unicorns from the hoofball team stopped by the table and said cheery hellos to her.

"Can't wait to get that trophy tomorrow," said Blaze, a bright orange unicorn with a neon-yellow mane.

"You and Sapphire are sure going to give Glitterhorn a

big surprise!" a silver unicorn named Star squealed.

"Totally," Comet said, wondering if she believed it.

Comet groaned as they walked away. *That was close,* she thought. She had been keeping the baking competition to herself. She didn't want the team to find out and think she wasn't taking the secret ingredient plan seriously. Everyone on the team was so excited about her and Sapphire's secret move, and Comet had never felt so popular. It would have been nice, if she hadn't felt terrified that she was going to let them all down.

Shamrock waited until the hoofball group was out of earshot. "Baking?" he asked quietly. "I thought the baking club only met once a week."

"Yeah, you know," Comet said, thinking quickly, "and all the—uh—stress baking."

Shamrock nodded. "We have noticed how stressed you've been—"

"You've been talking about me behind my horn?"

"We've only been saying that we're worried about you!"

Comet felt like she had swallowed a lump of uncooked dough. "Shamrock, you don't know anything about this. Or hoofball!" She stomped on the floor with frustration.

The unicorn peeked over their stack of books to hiss, "I'm going to tell Professor Jazz on you!"

"Don't worry, I'm leaving!" Comet told them as she gathered the cookbooks from the floor. It felt like a kettle was whistling inside her. She wondered if smoke was coming out of her ears.

Shamrock's eyebrows disappeared behind his glasses frames as his face fell into a deep frown. "I'm sorry, Comet. I was only trying to help."

"Well, don't!"

Comet left the library with tears in her eyes. Shamrock didn't understand. She could totally handle it. She would show him.

7

Apple-Cider Doughnuts

Comet huffed and puffed past groups of students on the main lawn, where they were hanging out on blankets and eating snacks. *Must be nice.*

Comet was hustling toward her last practice with Sapphire and Flash. A couple of weeks earlier she would have been so excited to hang out with her best friend and the coolest unicorn in school. But hoofball was so not fun anymore. They just did the same thing over and over. And somehow it felt like Comet was getting worse. She could tell Sapphire was getting more and more disappointed in her. With a sigh, Comet dragged herself toward the practice field. *At least it's the last practice. Tomorrow I'll either make it work . . . or I won't.*

She made her way along a forest path, fallen leaves crunching beneath her hooves and the wind whistling through the trees. There was something about this weather that always made her want to make apple-cider doughnuts with fresh cider. Comet smiled, thinking she would ask Stella and Celest if they could make some tomorrow morning. *Maybe that would be a good idea for the competition cake,* she thought. She couldn't believe she hadn't thought of a cake yet. How could the next day be the last lesson before the competition? Comet had told Stella and Celest that she had already figured out a recipe and was just keeping it a surprise. It felt like she was lying to everyone, and she didn't know how much more of all this she could take. *It'll be over tomorrow,* she reminded herself.

"Comet! Over here!"

Comet looked up to see Twilight standing by a tree with her easel and paints all set up. Comet trotted over, wanting to see what her friend was creating.

The scene was of the forest, but the leaves were still green. There was a bright blue sky with a brilliant rainbow over the trees. She'd even included the top of the library's crystal towers and the red stables in the distance. The scene looked just like it had on Comet's first day of school.

"Wow, Twilight. I love all the colors you've used. It's beautiful."

"Thanks, Comet. I've been working on it for ages." Twilight laughed softly. "The leaves were still green when I started!"

"But what about sculpting with the art club?"

Twilight shrugged. "I'm terrible at it, but it's fun to hang out with other artists. It's just, sometimes I need to have some time alone, you know? This painting makes me feel calm. Like I'm exactly where I'm supposed to be when I

have a paintbrush." Twilight blushed. "Maybe that doesn't make any sense."

"No, it does! Baking is like that for me. Or it used to be at least."

"Used to be?"

Comet sighed. She looked at Twilight for a long time before deciding she couldn't keep it to herself any longer. "Can you keep a secret?"

"Um, I think so."

That was good enough for Comet. "I entered a baking competition against Glitterhorn. It's right after the hoofball match tomorrow. Stella and Celest have been giving me extra lessons." She looked at Twilight out of the corner of her eye, worried about what she would say.

"You're the best baker I know! You'll win for sure."

Comet smiled. "Well . . . if I do win, I get to compete in another round against kids from all over the five kingdoms. I can even bring three friends with me."

Twilight's eyes sparkled. "That would be amazing. And, you know, Sapphire has always wanted to travel. She would love to hear about this."

Comet shook her head. "No way. I think she cares more about hoofball right now than anything else. And she is already annoyed with me."

"But you've been practicing for hoofball every day!"

"And baking every morning before school, but I'm worried I'm getting worse at both. Yesterday I accidently made an explosion by mixing baking powder with some wrong ingredients. Then later at hoofball practice, I couldn't even get my hoof to hit the ball!" Comet took a breath. She had been trying so hard to bottle all these feelings up, and now they were bursting out. *Kinda like my baking fail yesterday*, she thought. "I feel like I'm lying to everyone. Especially Sapphire. What would she say?"

Twilight paused to think. She always chose her words wisely. Comet admired that about her. For Comet, words tumbled out of her mouth like apples from a ripped bag.

"She knows how much you love baking," Twilight finally said. "And I think she would love the chance to travel somewhere. She might not be completely happy at first, but I think she'd understand and be excited in the end."

Comet considered this as she stared at Twilight's beautiful painting. It *was* calming. Feeling a little better, Comet thought, *Twilight's right. How could Sapphire be mad if I won the hoofball match and the baking prize?* She just had to win. Then she could tell Sapphire everything. "You're right. I can't let her down. Not in the hoofball game. And not with the baking prize."

"Comet, I didn't mean—"

But the final class bell interrupted her and reminded Comet where she was supposed to be.

"Oh no! I'm going to be late for practice. Thanks for talking with me, Twilight. This really helped. I just need to focus and do this. For Sapphire! For Unicorn University!"

"That's not really what I meant. . . ."

But Comet was already a rose-colored blur shooting toward the fields.

★

Comet skidded to a stop in front of Flash and Sapphire, accidently splattering them with mud. *Oops.*

"Hey, Comet," Flash said, looking at her mud-specked flanks. "Let me go get some towels."

"Comet!" Sapphire groaned as Flash walked away. "You're late again! I can't believe—"

"I know, I know," Comet said, trying to cut Sapphire off before things got too heated. "But I ran into Twilight and we had a really good talk, and—"

"I just don't know where your horn's at, Comet! You are always late to practice. And then when you're here, you don't pay attention and—"

"Listen! I know I haven't been great, but I promise I'm here for you—"

"No, you listen!" Sapphire was shouting now. "I know you can be silly, but our move is my only chance to get into this game. And I really want to play! If I could fly and kick, I would. But I'm counting on you, Comet."

Comet froze. She didn't know what to say and could feel tears welling up. Not wanting Sapphire to see her cry, she ran down the field to get into position. "Okay, let's get started!" she yelled, her voice wavering just a little.

Sapphire scraped the ground with her hooves. "Comet! I'm—"

"Okay, let's go!" Flash blew a whistle. "We're running out of sunshine here."

Comet and Sapphire ran their special play over and over, but Comet kept messing up. First she couldn't even make herself float, which sometimes happened when she was feeling low. Then when she could float, she was all wobbly and couldn't kick the ball.

After what felt like the millionth try, Sapphire ran over to Comet.

"Hey, Comet, is this because of what I said? I'm really sorry. Sometimes my competitive side gets the best of me. You're doing great, I promise."

"Okay, you two!" Flash yelled from across the field. "Final goal before the Glitterhorn game!" She kicked the ball toward the goal, but it veered close to Sapphire and Comet. Sapphire leapt up and kicked the ball toward the goal. Score!

"Wow, Sapphire," said Comet. "I don't think you guys need me. Maybe tomorrow—"

But Sapphire interrupted her. "I do need you, Comet! We're partners. I'm sorry I wasn't fair before."

Flash ran over to them before Comet could say anything else. "Don't worry, Comet. I think it's just nerves. You'll do better tomorrow," Flash told her. "Let's go get some dinner."

8

Biscuits and Candied Apples

It was Saturday morning, and the whole school was getting ready for Glitterhorn's arrival. Comet walked through the main lawn as students hung up a welcome banner and set up tents. The Sparklers, the school band, tuned their instruments onstage as the dancing club warmed up for their routine. The whole school felt alive, and everyone seemed so excited.

For the first time in her life, Comet felt like she wanted to run away from the crowd. She wished she could go back to her stable and hide in her stall all day. In her team uniform—a short cape with the letters *UU* stitched onto the back—she looked the part of a hoofball player, but she felt like a fraud.

Comet forced herself to walk to the school kitchen for one more morning lesson. She had no idea how she would admit that she didn't have a plan for the competition cake. It was just that every time she thought about it, she would get a wave of nerves and would start to worry about disappointing people. So she had kept putting it off. And now she was out of time.

The sight of the chimney smoke did make her smile, if only a little. It always made her feel at home. Comet pushed open the big wooden door and was met with a surprise.

Shamrock, Twilight, Stella, and Celest were all gathered around the table. There were apple-oat muffins, biscuits, and candied apples piled high in front of them.

"You're finally here!" Celest cheered.

"We came to surprise you!" Twilight said. "I told

Shamrock what's been going on. I'm sorry I didn't keep your secret, Comet. But I figured you needed all the support you could get." Twilight shimmered a little, becoming invisible and then visible again. Like Comet, Twilight found that her ability to control her special power could be swayed by her emotions.

"Thank you for telling him, Twilight," Comet told her honestly. "I wish I had told you both earlier. You could've helped!"

Comet had tears in her eyes. She was overwhelmed by all the love in this little room. She gave Shamrock a hug, hanging her head over his neck and squeezing him tight. "I'm sorry I've been so rude!"

Shamrock just shook his head. "Don't even worry about it."

"And look! The doughnuts are ready!" Stella turned toward her from the oven, carrying a tray of freshly baked treats.

Everyone dug into the food, and Comet was grateful no one mentioned any kind of competition. As she looked around the table of treats, Comet was suddenly struck with an idea. "I know what I'm going to bake today!" she shouted to the room.

Stella and Celest looked at each other with raised eyebrows. Comet realized they'd known all along that she hadn't had a plan. She couldn't help but laugh.

"Twilight, do you think you can coordinate with the sculpting club before the baking contest?" Comet asked.

"We have a booth set up and we're giving demonstrations. What do you need?"

Comet filled them in on her plans. Everyone was on board.

"Now I think it's time you get to that hoofball match," Celest reminded her with a wink when everything was settled.

"We'll bring all the supplies!" Stella boomed as Comet dashed out the door.

Comet left the kitchen feeling better than she had in weeks. She even managed to fly the whole way without running into anything!

9

The Real Secret Ingredient

The field didn't look like the stretch of grass and goals Comet had come to know. The simple wooden goals had been shined and polished so that they sparkled in the morning light, and a brand-new net hung between the posts. The grass was freshly cut, and freshly painted wooden stands had been put up so that more unicorns could watch the game.

The Glitterhorn team practiced on one side of the field. True to their name, each player had a special glittering sleeve over their horn with a sparkling letter *G*. Comet was suddenly worried. They seemed so much more serious than Unicorn U.

"Comet! Comet!" Coach waved her over to the team huddle.

"I have a little surprise for the team," Flash was saying as Comet joined the circle. Using her horn, Flash opened a bag. Inside were tons of purple bandannas, just like Flash's! "I thought we could all wear them for the game!"

The team cheered and helped each other loop the bright fabric around horns and tie back manes. Everyone had a different style, but they still looked like a team. Comet stood just outside the huddle, looping her bandanna around her ankle. She thought the team looked super cool, and everyone looked so happy. But she couldn't help feeling like she was an outsider looking in. She tried to shake off the feeling and get her head in the game.

Soon the referee blew the whistle to signal it was time to play, and everyone took their places. Comet and Sapphire waited on the sidelines together. Usually they would be whispering and giggling as they watched, but neither of them said anything. Comet felt like the air was buzzing with all the things she wanted to admit to her friend.

Flash bedazzled the other team by turning her mane from pink to purple to teal and got the ball from the first ball toss. Before the other team knew what was happening, she ran the ball down the field and scored! The crowd went wild, but Comet couldn't stop looking at the clock. If the game went into overtime, she'd miss the start of the baking competition. She floated up just a little to see the tops of the baking tent, and wondered what was going on inside it.

The other team was back on their hooves fast, working together to pass the ball to each other so quickly that the Unicorn U players could barely keep track. Glitterhorn swept past all the lines of defense and scored.

Coach called Sapphire and Comet over.

"Time to add our secret ingredient!" Flash told them

with a wink. "You guys can do this! Don't worry about yesterday."

Comet felt like her hooves were stuck in the mud, as if her whole body were telling her not to go. She looked over to Sapphire and saw that her friend was feeling totally different. It looked like Sapphire was shining from the inside out as she did a little excited prance along the sidelines.

"This is our moment! I want to remember this feeling forever," Sapphire cheered.

Comet never wanted to feel this way again. *I wish I could feel like Sapphire, but it feels like my heart is split in two*, she thought. And just like that, Comet knew what she had to do. She hoped everyone would understand.

"Actually, Coach," Comet said, her voice wavering a little. She could feel the whole team's eyes on her. "Sapphire is your secret ingredient, not me."

Coach looked away from the field to stare at Comet. "What do you mean?"

"Yeah, Comet, what do you mean?" Sapphire looked totally confused. Everyone did.

Comet could hear the cheers from the unicorns on the sidelines and knew she was making the right decision. She took a deep breath.

"Your secret weapon is Sapphire's perfect kick. All I do is float. And honestly, I'd probably mess up. My heart isn't on the field today. It's in the baking tent. I've been trying to

live up to your expectations, Sapphire, instead of listening to my heart. And it's taken me away from what I really love."

Sapphire looked stunned. "Huh? What baking tent?"

"You don't need me, Sapphire," Comet told her. "You have the best kick on the whole team, and you can jump higher than anyone else. Have Flash kick it to you a little high, and jump and kick like yesterday. I know you guys can do it. Way better than I ever could. This is *your* moment, Sapphire."

Sapphire just shook her head with surprise.

Comet turned away from her teammates. She didn't want to see their faces as she dashed away from the field. She knew she had made the right decision. She hoped they would see it too.

10

The Last-Minute Cake

Comet could see the baking tent. It was made of billowing white fabric, with flags perched atop three points of the tent. They waved merrily in the distance. Comet dashed toward them, finally ready for her own moment to shine.

Inside the tent, the baking club surrounded the Unicorn University table, with Twilight and Shamrock.

A golden unicorn stood at the other table. Like the Glitterhorn hoofball team, he was wearing a glittering horn cover with a sparkling *G* in the center. Comet looked down at the purple bandanna tied around her ankle and tried not to think about what her team must have been feeling right then.

An older unicorn with wire-rimmed glasses and a pink beret walked into the center of the tent. "Welcome, bakers." Her voice was sweet and kind. She reminded Comet of her grandmother. "My name is Terry Strawberry, and I'm here to judge this honored tradition. I remember competing in it myself, when I was still in school."

Comet had never thought about this baking competition as a tradition—no one talked about it like they talked about the hoofball match. There wasn't a case of trophies in the library or anything. Comet wondered how many students in the history of the school had entered, and if any of them had made the same mistakes she had.

"As you know, today you will be making a cake that best represents your school. I am looking forward to seeing what you've developed. You have one hour. Ready, set, bake!"

Comet stared at her workstation. She was reminded of

something Twilight had once told her, how a blank canvas was always the scariest. She looked at her friends and smiled. She knew just what to do. She had a plan, even if it was a last-minute one.

Soon the smells of the tent pulled her into her baking zone, and it felt like she was back in Stella and Celest's kitchen before all the baking competition and hoofball match business had begun. Back when she would stop by

just to see what they were cooking and if they would let her help. As if on cue, Stella yelled, "You can do it, Comet!"

"Shh, she's in the zone!" Celest said, trying to quiet Stella down.

Comet got to work, mixing the different doughs and frostings with her hooves. She tasted her cake mixtures and added more sugar here, and more butter there.

Time raced by, but she managed to get her cake layers into the oven in time. She was just finishing her decorations when she heard Terry Strawberry say, "Step away from your tables, bakers. Time is up."

Comet took a deep breath and looked at her cake, happy with knowing that she'd done her best.

11

The Flavors of
Unicorn University

I made a crystalized sugar cake," the Glitterhorn baker explained as he presented his creation. "I chose this because I wanted it to glitter in the sunshine, just like Glitterhorn College!"

Comet thought the only word to describe his creation was "spectacular." The cake sparkled as if it were covered in diamonds.

Terry Strawberry sliced into the cake, cutting into the big letter *G* he had made out of powdered sugar in the center. "It certainly glitters, and is very sweet. Well done, Nova."

Comet's heart beat inside her chest. She wondered if she had made the wrong choice. *No turning back now.*

Comet looked down at her cake. She had draped over it the purple bandanna Flash had given her at the start of the game.

"I covered the cake in this bandanna because it represents the Unicorn University hoofball team, which our whole school is proud of. I wanted the bandanna to be the first thing people see because the team is often front and center at school."

Using her teeth, Comet pulled off the bandanna to reveal a tall cake covered with green frosting. On the top were the tiny sculptures Twilight and the art club had made. There were

a few little red barns, and there was a miniature version of the Crystal Library. The art club had even managed to create tiny trees.

"The outside of the cake is our campus, a beautiful place that all of us at Unicorn U have come to call home. I know we all think it's as magical as a rainbow. Miss Strawberry, would you mind slicing into the cake?"

"Of course not," she replied, her eyes sparkling behind her glasses. She sliced to reveal many different layers all stacked up on top of one another. The inside looked just like a rainbow.

"I layered lots of different flavors inside the cake. There's an apple-cider layer, an orange-and-cinnamon layer, and a candied-apple layer. Because Unicorn U has so many talented students. There's the baking club and dance club, the Sparklers and the science club. We're all different in our own ways, but together we make Unicorn University."

Terry Strawberry took a bite and chewed. It seemed to

Comet that she took way more time on this one that she had on Nova's. *Is that a good sign or a bad sign?* Comet worried.

"This is delicious, Comet. I especially like the orange-and-cinnamon layer. You both made wonderful desserts, and it's hard for me to declare a winner today in this tent. But I have been swayed by your creativity and heart, Comet. This cake has more personality than most. Congratulations. You have won the baking competition for Unicorn University!"

A big chorus of cheers surprised Comet, and she looked over to see the whole hoofball team standing at the sides of the tent. Comet could see that Flash was with the hoofball trophy. And there was Sapphire, cheering more loudly than anyone else.

12

As Sparkly As a
Sugar Doughnut

R eady, Comet?" Sapphire asked from outside her stall. It was the morning after the big day with Glitterhorn.

"As ready as I'll ever be," Comet said, her hoofball cape slung over her shoulder.

Sapphire and Comet walked toward the hoofball field. Comet was going to return her uniform to Coach. She was going to need to focus on baking, with the Five Kingdoms Bakeoff coming up. The two friends walked quietly, neither knowing quite what to say.

"Comet—"

"Sapphire—"

The two started laughing. By talking at the same time, they had somehow broken the spell that had kept them silent.

"Me first," Comet said. "I should have told you the truth. I know that now."

Sapphire shook her head. "I wasn't listening. I should've known something was up. It's just, I thought I wouldn't be able to play without you. I thought Coach only wanted me because I was paired up with you."

Comet nudged her friend gently with her flank. "I know how doubting yourself feels. Let's agree to never keep things from each other again."

That was a promise Comet knew she could keep.

As simple as that, the two unicorns were okay once more. Comet felt as sparkly as a sugar doughnut.

When Comet arrived at the Friendly Fields, she was

surprised to see not only Coach but the whole hoofball team gathered together, and even Shamrock and Twilight stood off to the side.

Comet looked at Sapphire with surprise. "What's going on?"

Sapphire shook her head. "I have no clue."

Comet looked over to Shamrock and Twilight, but they shrugged, clearly also confused.

Just then the whole team jumped up and yelled, "Surprise!" They had strung up a banner that said, GO, BAKERS, GO!

Flash came to the front of the group and held out four aprons. She called Shamrock and Twilight over and draped an apron over each of the four friends' necks, as if the aprons were special garlands at the end of a winning game. "We know you're not on the hoofball team anymore, Comet, but we wanted you to know we are still cheering for you and your team of bakers!"

Comet felt so happy that her hooves floated right off the grass. For the first time ever, she didn't know what to say. Until finally she managed, "Go, Unicorn University!"

About the Author and the Illustrator

Daisy Sunshine writes books and dreams of unicorns by the sea in Santa Cruz, California.

Monique Dong is an illustrator whose passion is creating images that encompass light, life, warmth, and color. She had her start in animation before making the jump into the world of illustration. She lives in South Africa with her husband and two very busy little boys, Felix and Bailey.